Stark, A Harry Stark Mystery

by

John Worsley Simpson

Stark, A Harry Stark Mystery

Cover Art by *Debbie Taylor*

The Wild Rose Press, Inc.
PO Box 708
Adams Basin, NY 14410-0708
Visit us at www.thewildrosepress.com

Publishing History
First Edition, 2022
Trade Paperback ISBN 978-1-5092-4029-6
Digital ISBN 978-1-5092-4030-2

Previously Published, 2017, MuseItUp Publishing
Published in the United States of America

The body was slumped over the desk. Blood ran like a crimson ribbon down both sides of the neck from a tear in the scalp somewhere in the occipital region above the hairline. You couldn't see the wound, and you couldn't tell that the skull was crushed beneath the ruptured skin.

Above the dead man, on the wall, hung a framed cover of Financial Post magazine: the person on the cover unusually young and oddly dressed. The heading was "The Midas Touch," so right away you'd put Financial Post and "The Midas Touch" together, and you'd expect to see a picture of an older businessman or some hotshot wunderkind buyout artist. But the picture on the magazine's cover was of a kid.

He was grinning, a little sheepish and yet a little cocky, a gee-whiz kid posing for a picture he knew his mom would see. This kid was no high-rolling stock promoter, no big deal-maker, not even a market-busting entrepreneur. He was a geologist and a genius, and the Midas touch referred to his success at finding treasure hidden by nature deep within the earth that glowed and clinked and made him, but mostly made the people he worked for, a hell of a lot of money. His name was Chris Harper, and young Chris would never be posing for another magazine cover, or any other picture his mother would see. His face lay on the keyboard of his computer, and he would never grin again.

Praise for John Worsley Simpson

"Simpson's crafty plotting, together with his easy command of the book's characters and Toronto locales, makes this a must read. This has all the hallmarks of an enduring series."

~ John North, Toronto Star

Chapter One

The body was slumped over the desk. Blood ran like a crimson ribbon down both sides of the neck from a tear in the scalp somewhere in the occipital region above the hairline. You couldn't see the wound, and you couldn't tell that the skull was crushed beneath the ruptured skin.

Above the dead man, on the wall, hung a framed cover of *Financial Post* magazine: the person on the cover unusually young and oddly dressed. The heading was "The Midas Touch," so right away you'd put *Financial Post* and "The Midas Touch" together, and you'd expect to see a picture of an older businessman or some hotshot wunderkind buyout artist. You'd expect the right uniform: the dark suit, maybe a bright Paisley tie, the perfectly styled haircut. But the picture on the magazine's cover was of a kid.

He'd been twenty-seven at the time the photograph was taken, in August 1992, four years and nearly five months before the present day, but he looked eighteen. The man wore a Tilley hat and the whole Tilley bush outfit, shirt and pants. The hat was pushed back on his head, and his blond hair hung stringy over his forehead, finger-combed at best. He was grinning, a little sheepish and yet a little cocky, a gee-whiz kid posing for a picture he knew his mom would see. This kid was no high-rolling stock promoter, no big deal-maker, not even a market-busting entrepreneur. He was a geologist and a genius, and the Midas touch referred to his success at finding treasure hidden by nature deep within the earth that glowed and clinked and made him, but mostly made the people he worked for, a hell of a lot of money. His name was Chris Harper, and young Chris would never be posing for another magazine cover, or any other picture his mother would see. His face lay on the keyboard of his computer, and he would never grin again.

****

Over the last decade or so Chilly had taken on a new status, moving up in the world to the rank of "homeless person." Chilly liked that description. "It's what you call a concept, really," he once told his pal Booger. It was a lot better than "wino" or "bum" or "derelict," the names he used to be called. Chilly had been on the streets for a long time. It wasn't so much the "homeless" part of the term he liked: it was the word "person." He *was* a person, after all. Of course he was a person. He knew he was a person. His mother—if she was still alive back in Antigonish—knew he was a person. Or maybe she didn't. (Chilly laughed inside at that.) She sure as hell *used* to know it, but then he hadn't spoken to her in—what?—fifteen, no, more like twenty years. And she probably thought he was nothing but worm feed by now, or probably *she* was. "We'll all be worm feed in the end, Horace, rich and poor alike," she used to say. Well, Chilly hadn't become worm feed yet. Chilly was a survivor. "You're a survivor, Chilly. You'll outlive us all," Booger had told him that one time when Chilly's face was a mass of blood, his mouth torn up so badly he couldn't speak, after a couple of punks had put the boots to him in an alley near St. Michael's Hospital. Kicked him so hard, he'd had to eat through a straw for weeks after, and pissed blood. He had a jagged scar across his left eye and down his cheek and fuzzy vision in that eye. He still walked with a limp.

"Bastards. Little punks, skinny," he'd told Booger after he'd got out of hospital. "A few years back, when I was in the Navy, I'd a bounced the two of 'em off the walls of that alley like god-damned ping-pong balls, Booger. I tell ya, I would."

"Don't get your balls in a knot, Chilly. Ferget it. Yer back on yer feet now. Yer a survivor."

"How the hell do you get your *balls* in a knot, you stupid ass? Yer always buggering up expressions like that, Booger. What the hell's the matter with ya?"

A street social worker had reminded Chilly recently of his standing as a person and the awareness of his status had led him to think about trying to sell the credit cards. Not long ago, he'd have kept the money in the wallet and thrown away the cards. The money was immediate, hard, real. You could hold it, count it and know its worth and exactly how much booze it would buy you. To Chilly, credit cards were nothing but useless pieces of plastic. You could sell them to druggies and that, but not without complications. First, you had to find a druggy. And not just any druggy. That'd be stupid. He, or even she, would have to be small and weak. And the person couldn't be a schizo. You'd have to be able to have a reasonable discussion with him. Then you had to hope that he had money.

There were two problems there. The obvious one: if the guy didn't have money, he couldn't buy the cards. And two: if there was no money, the druggy might try to take the cards off you, and even the weak ones—

especially if they were slightly schizo, which they mostly all were—could get fired-up strong, and they could always pull a knife on you. And even without all that, you had to go through all the bargaining shit, and you didn't know what to ask, and you didn't know whether you were being ripped off. It had always been too much of a pain in the ass for Chilly. But these days—well, it helped him prove he was, as they said, a *person,* to take all that time and trouble. Sort of like—you know, a businessman.

Chapter Two

Their friends and relatives thought Chris Harper and Dianne Johnson were the perfect couple, but his mother didn't. She didn't like the fact that Chris was expected to share the cooking and the housework; and she didn't like it that Dianne had her own career as a marketing consultant; and that Dianne used her unmarried name, Johnson, and refused to have children until Chris stopped spending six months of the year trudging across frozen tundra or plodding through steaming jungles.

Dianne wanted to have children, but not under those circumstances. "I'm not raising kids with a part-time father," she said. And so they carried on largely separate lives. Not that they didn't want to be together. They saw most things the same way, had the same liberal attitudes, saw themselves as progressive, egalitarian.

They enjoyed each other's company. When they'd got married, they'd both agreed that the Beaches was the perfect place to live, with lovely old homes, full of like-minded people, lots of comfortable cafés and fun places to eat.

As soon as they saw the apartment on Carson Avenue, the upper floor of an immense converted Victorian-style house built in the 1920s, they both knew immediately this was the place for them. With four bedrooms and a den and a living room and formal dining room and a large kitchen, it had everything they wanted.

There was a garage at the back and a fire escape. Dianne liked the idea of living on the second floor. She felt more secure—important with Chris's being away so much. There was a burglar-alarm system and lots of smoke detectors, and Chris installed a carbon-monoxide detector as well.

When Chris was home, they alternated the cooking chores, or they ate out. In fact, they had that down to a regular pattern. On Mondays, she cooked; on Tuesdays, he cooked; on Wednesdays, they ate out. That pattern repeated for Thursday, Friday and Saturday, and they usually ate at her parents' on Sunday.

Once a month, they'd drive north to his mother's house in Gravenhurst, in their Honda Civic, a sensible small car that used less of the world's oil reserves. They owned only one car between them, to minimize the pollutants they regretted having to put into the atmosphere.

Each had a bicycle, lightweight alloy, Italian, with a price tag of fifteen hundred dollars. Inside the garage, at the rear, a massive steel cupboard with a highly secure lock contained their camping equipment, thousands of dollars' worth of the best the Mountain Equipment Co-op had to offer.

Holidays were always spent camping. Their last summer vacation had been a three-week bicycle tour of England and Scotland. Chris liked good beer and single-malt Scotch. They made their own wine and drank it with every meal, which nearly always included pasta. They had a seven-hundred-and-fifty-dollar, gleaming, chrome-and-black-lacquer espresso maker, and when Chris finished working on his computer every evening, he would make cappuccinos for both of them.

Dianne's sister, Jennifer, found Chris lying on his computer keyboard. She had a key to the apartment, and when no one answered the bell, she had let herself in. The car was in the driveway, so she figured they must have just run around the corner to the store.

Jennifer was an engineer, a very practical, level-headed person, with an analytical mind, so as soon as she saw Chris, she sized up the situation immediately, and without touching anything else, still wearing gloves against the January cold and snow, she picked up the phone and dialled 911. Dianne was in the apartment when Jennifer found Chris. When she heard Jennifer's voice, she cried out for help. Jennifer froze for an instant, and then looked for something to use as a weapon.

There was a gas fireplace in the den with an antique set of fireplace tools beside it. She picked up a poker and went warily looking, fearing the intruder might still be there, and that maybe he had her sister on one of the beds to rape her.

But Dianne's cries came from the kitchen. Jennifer looked carefully around the edge of the doorway, but the room was empty. Dianne called out again. "I'm in here." The voice came from the pantry in the corner of the room. The door was locked and bolted, the key lying on the floor a few feet away. Jennifer unlocked the door, slid back the bolts, and Dianne fell out into her arms.

"Oh my God. Oh my God," Dianne sobbed.

****

Constable Homer Wingate and his partner, Joyce Lee, heard the call on the radio when they were only a couple of blocks away from Carson Avenue. They worked out of 55 Division, their beat including the Beaches. Homer flicked on the flashers and made a U-turn on Queen in front of the Beaches Library at Kew Beach, bouncing the right front wheel of the scout car on to the sidewalk in the process. Joyce glared at him and snapped on the siren. Homer's head jerked toward her. He turned the siren off. "We don't need that," he said.

"Yes, we do." Joyce flicked the siren on again. Homer shook his head. They pulled up in front of the Harper-Johnson house in less than a minute, sliding on a patch of ice and grazing a tree with the corner of the bumper.

Joyce had the door open before the car had stopped, and was out and running toward the house, drawing her gun as she went, while Homer was still turning off the siren. By the time he caught up with her, Joyce was already halfway up the inside stairs. Joyce always went first. Homer didn't object—partly because it wouldn't do any good, and partly because he wasn't the bravest person in the world. If Joyce wanted to be the target, that was her choice.

Joyce didn't go first for some psychological or emotional reason; not even because she had something to prove as a five-foot-ten Chinese-Canadian cop. Joyce went first because she knew she was a better cop than Homer—tougher, a better shot, and stronger than he was. And she had a sharper mind, so that as soon as she saw the way Jennifer held Dianne, she knew right away there wouldn't be an intruder lurking around a corner, and she holstered her gun. Homer still had his drawn, and Joyce made an impatient gesture, telling him to put it away. Other cars were screeching to a halt in front of the building.

"Go down and tell them to cool it," she told Homer, who, despite the fact that he was the senior partner, did as ordered.

****

Homer was one of the few cops Harry Stark liked. It should have been awkward that Stark didn't like many cops, since Stark was a detective. But Stark didn't have anything against cops as *cops.* He just didn't like the people who became cops. If he'd been a teacher or a lawyer or a truck driver, he wouldn't have liked his colleagues much either.

Stark was widely and grudgingly acknowledged to be one of the most successful investigators on the force, and he was respected and to a degree even admired for that. Stark lived in the Beaches, and he often had coffee with Homer and Joyce in Holtzman's Deli, a few doors along Queen Street from Lick's. Stark liked Holtzman's because Sid Holtzman had a booth in the back corner that he used for making out his menus and for doing his bookkeeping and picking his horses from the *Toronto Sun*, and Sid let Stark sit there and smoke his Gauloises.

It was practically the only place in the Beaches where they didn't object to the pungent aroma of his French cigarettes. In Holtzman's you couldn't smell them over Sid's cigars anyway. Stark would sit in the back booth and skim the customers' newspapers that Sid would dump there. Stark didn't think much of the Toronto papers. The fact was, Stark didn't have much use for any newspapers anywhere. They dealt with what he had little interest in—the modern world. Stark almost exclusively read novels and histories of his preferred century, the nineteenth.

He didn't think much of Joyce. She was a good cop, fair and all that, but she was too straight. She never relaxed, and always seemed to be telling Homer it was time to get back on patrol. A couple of times he had come close to calling her Marge, which was what the other cops called her among themselves—but never to her face.

****

When Stark arrived at the Carson Avenue house, the place seemed like a movie shoot, with police-line tape strung from tree to tree along the front and down both sides of the house like a yellow fence. Everything glowed eerily in the glare of spotlights from the roofs of cars parked crazily, blocking the street, and from portable lights that had been set up at the rear of the building. Detective Carol Weems and her partner Detective Jim Cory from 55 Division were comparing notes on the verandah, both stepping from one foot to the other against the cold, their breath making billows of condensation. Stark flashed his badge at a rookie constable who held up a hand to stop him.

"Sorry, Sarge," the kid said sheepishly. As a detective, Stark's rank was equivalent to a uniformed sergeant. Cory looked up.

"You're back?" he said, surprised. Weems glared at Cory. "Of course, if you're back, they'd naturally put you on the case. You live around here, don't you? I didn't know you were back. Everything okay?"

Stark didn't answer.

"Hello, Harry, how are you this fine and frosty evening," Weems said, in an obvious change of subject, which might have been the reason for the lilt in her voice. On the other hand, Stark thought, it might have been a hint that she'd be happy to take the chill off him as she had on one other memorable occasion. He made a mental note, and then tried to remember why he'd never called her again, especially if it was that memorable. There was something—

"Shall we fill you in, Harry?" Cory broke off the memory search.

"What have you got?"

"One victim, male, Chris Harper, white, thirty years of age. Looks as if somebody tried to scramble his brains through the back of his head. Body was found by one—" he flipped a couple of pages in his notebook, "—Jennifer Johnson, sister of the victim's wife. *Her* name is—Dianne Johnson."

"Common-law?"

"No, just modern. He was an archaeologist or something."

"Geologist," Weems said.

"Whatever. An egghead. Hey, that's pretty funny. His egghead got cracked."

"That's really funny," Weems said, shaking her head.

"Your problem is you've got no sense of humour."

"Working with you, Cory—"

"Can we skip the juvenile banter?" Stark said, shaking his head.

"Sure. So the wife was locked in the pantry. She says she came home about four-forty-five this afternoon, and that somebody in a black balaclava grabbed her from behind as she went into the kitchen, put a gloved hand over her mouth, dragged her into the pantry and locked the door behind her."

"How did she know he wore a balaclava, and that it was black? I mean, if he—"

"From behind? Got a glimpse—"

"As he closed the door."

"You've read this?"

"Go on."

"That's about it. She figures she was in there about two hours before the sister came."

"Weapon?"

"No sign of anything. Something—heavy."

"Who'd you talk to, Weems?"

"Hey, wait a second—Harry." Cory interrupted, put out because he was the lead. "Sorry, but I've got—this is the information from both of us. The big thing is we got a footprint. The ident boys are out the back now, making a cast. You wanna see?"

Stark nodded, smiled at Weems. Cory started up the driveway toward the back of the house. Stark started to follow, then stopped short. The scout car lights didn't illuminate the whole of the narrow driveway. Toward the rear of the building, it was completely dark. Someone suddenly emerged from the blackness and an icy hand grabbed Stark's gut. For an instant, a small boy appeared to emerge from the dark and Stark felt sick. Then Weems brushed against him, and the boy became a policeman.

Weems's shoe caught a patch of ice, she slipped, but stopped herself from falling, letting out a high-pitched "whoo, whoo" that triggered in Stark's memory the reason he hadn't asked her out a second time. She was a screamer. That was it. He had nothing against an expression of exuberance at the moment of realization of the sought-after sensation, but Weems, he remembered, had been excessive. Not that he had any neighbours to worry about—his apartment was on Queen Street, above a dentist's office, which was closed in the evening. It was an end-unit, at the intersection of Gruen Avenue, and the adjacent apartment was above a bookstore, which used it for storage. Stark didn't object to enthusiasm in love-making, but Weems had made a noise that reminded him of a beagle he had as a kid that used to bay at the moon. But it wasn't just the volume and tonal quality of her display of satisfaction that had bothered him; on the face of it, it was flattering. It seemed so uncontrolled that it must have been genuine. But, he had thought, what if she had been faking? Then it would have meant she wasn't merely trying to make him feel that he had been a successful lover, but that she was actually taking the piss out of him.

There was a single, crisp footprint in the snow… New snow had fallen early that afternoon, so the print had to have been made since then. It had a deeply etched criss-cross pattern in an oblong shape with rounded ends between the heel and the sole.

"Looks like a hiking boot," Jim Cory said, sniffling. "What do you think?"

"So we're looking for a one-legged hiker?"

Cory screwed up his face. "The guy stepped in the snow with his right foot and then right on to the fire escape with his left foot."

"And when he came back, he had no feet?"

If Cory had been a rookie, he'd have been exasperated, but he just said flatly, "He could have gone out the front way."

"I doubt that."

"So do I. The thing is, if you try it, like I did, you'll see that when you come down the fire-escape stairs, the natural step takes you on to the paved driveway, and there's no snow there to show a print, because the guy downstairs, who owns the house—" Jim Cory consulted his notebook "—Roger Oates, he shovelled it. Actually, he's got one of those big Japanese jeep things—"

"Naturally."

"—with a plow hooked on the front. He does half the neighbourhood. He was a vice-president at a printing company. Got downsized. So now he runs a snowplow and makes birdhouses that he sells through a shop around the corner. They're pretty good, too. There's one—"

"Cory, forget the bloody birdhouses. What, did you get this guy's life history?"

"It's just that I—well, I make birdhouses, myself." Cory didn't see Weems silent snigger. "You know, it's sort of a hobby, so we got talking."

"Did he hear anything?"

"Tonight, you mean? Not about the birdhouses?"

"Jesus. Of course tonight."

"Naw, nothing unusual."

"Nothing unusual, but something?"

"No, nothing. He said he didn't hear anything."

"You just said he said he didn't hear anything unusual."

"Yeah, but—"

"What I want to know is, did you ask him whether he heard *anything?* Doors opening, people coming and going, cars arriving?"

"No—not exactly. I asked him—"

"Whether he'd heard anything unusual. Okay, never mind. Carol," he said pointedly as Cory's shoulders sagged, "I want *you* to tell me who all these people are. What they do for a living, what you know about them."

"Not that much, Harry," Weems began unpromisingly, and her assessment was borne out. "As Cory tried to say, the victim was a geologist. The wife is a marketing consultant—whatever that is. The neighbours didn't know them except to say hello. The people on the left had just moved in. On the right there's a widow who's lived in the house fifty years. She doesn't hear very well and her eyesight is poor. She said they were a nice couple, and that's all she knew. Doesn't even know their names. Oh, they both work—worked—out of the house, but he also had an office downtown. He has a partner. Here—" She copied the partner's name and the address in a little notepad, tore out the sheet and handed it to Stark, keeping her own leather-bound notebook intact in case it ever became evidence in a trial.

"Okay, we've got a footprint, must have been made today because of snowfall. Right. But how do we know it wasn't the wife who made it, or the husband?"

Cory looked smug. "Because it's a man's footprint, size nine, according to the Identification Unit guys, and there's no boot in the apartment that matches it."

"It's an odd-looking thing," Stark said. "Should be easy enough to trace."

Cory sighed. "Yeah. Do you want us to—right, I'll check it out." Cory smiled and nodded. "Do you want to go see the body?"

"Yeah, let's get inside. It's bloody cold out here."

They climbed the fire escape stairs and entered the apartment through a small porch that had been glassed in, and in which you could have whiled away the summer hours in a rocking chair watching the birds, if there'd been room for a rocking chair, but there wasn't, most of the space being occupied by two expensive-looking bicycles, running shoes and ski boots and other outdoors gear and a full crate of bottles of homemade wine.

A long hallway ran to the centre of the apartment, the first doorway on the left giving entrance to the master bedroom; the next doorway, on the right, opened into the guest bedroom. There was a bathroom on the left, and the second doorway on the right led to the office. They could see the former whiz-kid geologist slumped over the keyboard of his computer. Marv Greenberg, from the coroner's office, stood with his arms folded, glaring impatiently. He started to say something, but Stark put up his hand. The computer screen was dark, the computer shut down, but a little green light glowed on the monitor, showing that it was still turned on.

"Who shut this off?" Stark said sharply. "Who turned off the computer?"

"I did." The voice, a woman's, came from another room. Stark followed the sound into the kitchen. The speaker, Jennifer Johnson, was sitting at the table with her arm around her sister. Joyce Lee was standing awkwardly with her back against the sink. She nodded to the sergeant without smiling.

"You are?" Stark asked the woman who had called out.

"Jennifer Johnson. I'm—this is my sister. I'm sorry. It was the only thing I touched, and I was wearing gloves. There was nothing on the screen, just a blank document file. I didn't think—"

"Never mind," Stark said in a clipped manner. He looked at Dianne Johnson. Her head was resting on her arms. She was shaking. He went back into the room where the body was and closed the door behind him.

It was a fully furnished office, divided into his and hers. Two computers—his and hers, two phones, a laser printer, a scanner, a fax machine, a photocopier. From the centre of the room to the left, the walls were covered with maps and charts; on the walls to the right of centre were advertising posters, pictures of product packages, an award from *Marketing* magazine to Dianne Johnson of Power, Short and Grammick Advertising for the best consumer print campaign of 1990.

"So what's the story, Marv?"

"Hey, listen, I've got places to go, people to see. I've signed your paper. Now, what do you want to know?"

"What killed him?"

"How should I know? There's no weapon."

"Come on, Marv."

"Something crushed the back of his skull. He was sitting there working on the computer and bango."

Stark bent over the body, studied the boyish face. "You clean out his pockets?"

Cory answered. "The stuff's bagged."

"I'll want to see it."

"Of course."

"So what are we looking for, Marv, a club, butt of a gun, iron bar?"

"I can't tell you that yet, not till the autopsy. It looks like something wide and heavy, rather than narrow and sharp. That's about all I can say."

"Lot of force, have to be a man?"

"I would say probably, yes."

"How many times was he hit? In anger, somebody smashing away, several blows?"

"Not likely. There would have been more blood spatter, some on the computer screen perhaps, and I couldn't imagine him being slumped over like that if someone had pounded at him. I would think he'd have fallen on the floor. No, this was one big swinging smash, with something pretty heavy. That's my guess."

"Like a baseball bat?"

"That would be the force of the blow, all right, but not a baseball bat—I don't think. This looks wider—maybe six inches or more."

"Mmm. And there's nothing around here that could have been used?"

"Ask your people."

"No, we didn't find anything," Jim Cory said.

"How long dead?"

"Six hours maybe."

"Thanks."

The coroner gave a mirthless smile and hurried out.

An ident officer asked Stark, "I'm through with this guy if you are. By the way, there's something a bit odd under the desk here."

"What's that?" Stark said.

"It's damp. It's wet, like water's been spilled, but there's no glass."

Stark got down on the desk and felt the dampness. "You're sure it's water?"

"There's no smell to it. It's not pee. I'll snip a piece of the carpet and test it."

"Okay. Just a sec, and they can take this guy away." Stark studied the body from various angles and examined the wound. Finally, he said, "Yeah. They can take him."

The ident officer nodded to two attendants from the body-removal firm contracted to do this work for the Toronto force. They brought in a white, plastic body bag, opened it on the floor, laid Chris Harper on it and zipped it shut. Stark hated the sound. He shivered. The ident officer put a seal on the bag, copied down the number on the seal. The body was put in a black cloth bag, lifted on to a Gurney and wheeled out.

"Who's following the body to CFS?" Stark asked,

referring to the Centre of Forensic Science, where the autopsy would be performed.

"I detailed a scout car to go with them," Cory said. "Do you want to talk to the wife, Harry?"

"Not yet. Let me see what he had in his pockets." Weems brought a plastic bag in from the hallway and handed it to Stark. Their hands touched and they exchanged flickering smiles. Stark put the evidence bag on a desk and examined the contents through the clear plastic. A set of keys, three subway tokens, a dollar-sixty-three in coins.

"No wallet?"

"Wallet's missing," Cory said. "Wife said he always carried a wallet, a hip wallet, an in-your-pants wallet, not an in-your-jacket wallet."

"Couldn't have left it on the dresser?"

"We searched the place thoroughly. There's no wallet here."

"What else is missing?"

"Looks like that's it. Course, she hasn't had a chance to check really. But her jewelry is all there, not that there's much of it. But there is a gold watch, and a chain with a gold nugget on it, which apparently is real."

"So somebody breaks in and kills the guy for his wallet?"

"Maybe he panicked. The wife said she shouted a lot and banged on the door of the pantry. Nobody heard her, but maybe he figured somebody would and he ran out the back door."

"How much money was in the wallet? Did she say?"

Weems answered, "I don't think we asked her. On the other hand, if he'd had, say, a couple of thousand in it, surely she would have said something. You don't want to interview her?"

"No, you've—she's gone through enough. You got the nuts and bolts. What's in this other evidence bag, photographs? What are these?"

"They were on the floor," the ident guy said, "scattered around. Probably they were on the desk, or something, and they got bounced off when the victim's head hit. Probably nothing, but they were out of place, so we bagged 'em."

"Okay," Stark said, turning to Weems. "I assume you put an alert out for this balaclava guy with the hiking boots?"

"Yeah, we've got officers cruising the neighbourhood, checking the bars and stores. Excuse me, Harry, but are you it? I mean from Homicide? It's just that we're short-staffed and, usually Homicide—"

"Homicide is also short-staffed. And we've got that triple in the West End."

"The three teenagers."

"Don't worry about it. You can call your people off in a couple of hours. They're not going to find anybody now. Concentrate on the weapon. Something that size'd be hard to hide. Look under bushes and in every garbage can for a couple of blocks. He wouldn't carry it far. Unless he had a car. Any tire tracks?"

Cory shook his head.

"Did you look in the garbage?"

"Sure, we emptied all the garbage cans in the neighbourhood."

"*You* did? Personally?" Stark raised an eyebrow.

"Well—"

"Did you look through the garbage in the house here?"

"Yep. There's only one container with anything in it, and that's in the kitchen."

"Let's have a look."

Cory shrugged. "You want to do that while the wife's in the kitchen?"

"No, you're right. Get the thing and bring it in here."

"Maybe you should go in there, Weems. You're a woman."

Weems sighed and shook her head, but she went into the kitchen and brought out the garbage can and, thoughtfully, a green plastic garbage bag. "I thought you could empty it out on this."

Stark tipped the contents of the can onto the plastic bag. He took out a pencil and poked through tea bags and coffee grinds, beer bottle caps and tissues, chicken bones and pizza crusts, two slices of burnt toast, a cotton string shopping bag that had been torn, four crumpled pieces of note paper that Stark flattened out. One read, "Jennifer called. Call her back." Two others were shopping lists. The fourth had been squeezed into a tiny ball. On it a large "X" had been made by repeated strokes of a pen. Other repeated strokes had formed a heavy circle around the "X." At the bottom of the paper, it said, "B. 4:15" Stark asked Weems for an evidence bag, and put the sheet of paper in it.

Cory shook his head. "Do you think that means something? Looks like a doodle to me."

"A pretty angry doodle, I'd say." Stark wrapped up the rest of the trash in the plastic bag and put it in the can. "Okay. Put this back when they leave. Where's she going to stay?" He jerked a thumb in the direction of the kitchen.

"With the sister." Weems flipped open her

notebook, took one of her cards from her pocket, copied Jennifer Johnson's address and handed Stark the card. In addition to the sister's address, there were three phone numbers, one marked "home," one marked "work" and one marked "mine." Stark looked at her and she looked back. Neither smiled. He put the card in his shirt pocket.

"What about a key to this place?"

"Here." Jim Cory took a key from his jacket pocket. "It's the sister's."

"Okay. Say, what's the mess in the kitchen?"

"Oh yeah," Cory answered, "the sister asked if she could clean it up before she left. I said no."

"You did right. I don't want anybody to touch anything. Did they have a party in here?"

"He did, apparently. She was at some old school friend's in Ottawa. She says he had some friends over."

"So, when she got home this afternoon, was she just arriving from out of town, or had she been home and gone out shopping or something?"

"She says she just got back home."

"How'd she get here?"

"She took the car."

"Check whether she went where she says she did. And she must have had a suitcase."

"I guess so."

"So where is it? I didn't see it—in the hallway. It's not here."

"It's in the master bedroom," Weems said.

Stark pursed his lips and touched them with his right forefinger. "The big bedroom at the back of the apartment, in the corner opposite the office?"

"That's right."

"So, she walked past the office and put the suitcase

in the bedroom and then walked back down the hall to the kitchen without noticing that her husband—"

"She said the office door was closed. She was going to make him a drink first. She was at the kitchen counter when the guy grabbed her."

"From behind. Sneaked in on hiking boots. The hall floor creaks in two spots. Did you notice that?"

"Can't say that I did."

"He sneaks up on her, wearing hiking boots—I didn't notice any tracks. He stepped in the snow outside."

"It's fairly dry snow, and if she's clinking glasses, maybe running the tap, and maybe she did hear him, but he just moved fast and grabbed her before she turned around. We didn't ask her." Cory didn't seem to like the tone of Stark's questions.

"What about the alarm? There's an alarm. I saw the panel."

"The wife said they always had it shut off when they were in the house. Put it on when they went to bed, or when nobody was home."

"Okay." Stark looked around as if trying to see whether there was something he might have missed that he should ask about. Finally, he said, "All right, I'm going. You two wait here until everybody's out. Make sure you lock up. Make sure they put a tape over the back door and the inside door in the hallway. Oh yeah, one other thing. Why is there a lock on the pantry door?"

"I asked that," Cory said sharply. "Three locks, two of them are bolts, and then there's a key lock. It's old, a skelton key—"

"What kind of key?" Weems said, her eyebrows lifting.

"Skelton."

"Like Red Skelton, the comedian?" Stark chuckled. Cory didn't get it.

"You know, an old-fashioned key," Cory said. "The pantry used to be the top of another flight of stairs. It was for the servants or something. This used to be one big house, you know, in the old days."

"Maybe when they say they've got skeltons in the closet, they mean comedians, not *skeletons?*" Stark said to Weems with a wink.

"I don't get the joke," Cory snapped.

"Never mind, Cory. Anyway, we know about the lock. The door has two big slide-bolt locks on it, too, eh? They must have been really nervous about those *skeltons.*"

Weems sniggered. Cory glared at her. Stark tossed his hand in farewell.

"Thanks for the help. I'll be in touch. Tell the sister I'll want to talk to the wife tomorrow."

"When?" Weems asked.

"I've no idea," Stark said, covering his thick mat of salt-and-pepper-hair with the floppy Irish wool hat he'd doffed when he'd entered the apartment. He strode quickly down the hallway, through the office, glancing at the "his" computer, out the door and down the iron fire escape, noting that Cory had been right. It was a natural motion to step from the fire escape on to the cleared driveway.

A reporter with a television crew in front of the house shoved a microphone under Stark's chin, but he brushed by her.

Chapter Three

At the piano in Carbo's, Morty Greenwood had just started his second set when Stark came in. Not that Morty really had sets. He just played until he had to have a piss. As the evening wore on, he consumed more white wine, and his playing time—between micturitions—got shorter and shorter. On this occasion, Morty was distracted by two lithesome young men—what Morty would have called boys—sitting opposite him at the piano bar, which consisted of a wood-grained, plastic top in the shape of a grand piano rimmed with a roll of black vinyl in dire need of replacement. When Stark had moved into the area and discovered Carbo's, he had ignorantly made some comment about the grand piano's tone, which brought a derisive sneer from Morty.

"Grand piano, are you kidding, boy? You're joking, aren't you?"

"What are you talking about, Morty?"

"This is no bloody grand piano. The swine who owns this place would never fork out for a grand piano, not even a baby grand, which, incidentally, is what this would be, my musically-out-of-it friend. This is a bloody half-sized upright. It goes to here." Morty reached his hand out to touch the bar top about eighteen inches from the front of the piano. "And here and here." He touched both ends of the keyboard. "If this were a fucking grand piano, I could make real music on it."

"Sounds pretty good to me, Morty."

"Christ."

The "boys" with whom Morty was preoccupied were in their mid-thirties—"boys" to few in the bar beside Morty, a man of indeterminate age, and glowingly proud of the fact that no one had a clue just how old he was. People always politely guessed a lot younger when he prompted them, and it pleased him to believe their guesses were genuine. Morty's skin was fine and smooth, enhanced by a judicious application of pancake makeup. "It's such a pain in the ass when I take a youngster home, Harold," he once said. (He refused to call Stark, "Harry," calling it "a garage mechanic's name.")

"I can imagine."

"What? No, no, you dickhead. Ooo, that's not a pain."

"You're outrageous, Morty."

"Mmm, I know. What I meant was, I have to get up before they do, no matter how hung over I am, and put my face on. I don't want them to see me without it. Of course, it's no use if you don't have the skin to begin with, and I'm very careful. I have a special aloe vera formulation, and I never, *ever* go out in the blazing sun without number thirty screen and my panama. Besides the fact that the sun dries you up like a fucking prune, I couldn't take the chance. My skin is so fair and delicate, I'd be melanoma city if I went out unprotected."

"Morty, I just hope you don't go *in* unprotected."

Stark knew the smiles and coy looks directed at the "boys" would come to no more than flirtation. "I'm past all that sailor-boy shit, Harold. It's far too risky these days." Morty lived alone, but Stark knew he had a steady

26

boyfriend, George, an accountant, and regular secret flings with Carl, a vice-president with an auto-parts company, who lived with his wife and two of his four kids in Grosse Pointe, Michigan, and came to town two or three times a month.

Morty gave Stark a conspiratorial smile and a wink when Stark took his usual spot, the first stool on Morty's left, so he could look down and watch Morty's fingers dance over the keys, and where, later in the evening, after he'd switched from beer to scotch and smoked a pack of Players, (Ulysses Papalamdropoulos, the bar's owner, asked him not to smoke his Gauloises. "If this was Athens, no problem, but here—") He'd slip down beside Morty at the keyboard and sing a couple of numbers in a husky, but mellifluous, high baritone. And sometimes, if he weren't too pissed, it would mean all the difference in whether a new acquaintance would go home with him or not.

When Morty finished the piece he was playing, he stood up and put a hand on Stark's hand. "You okay?"

Stark looked uncomfortable. He nodded perfunctorily and started to pull his hand away, but he realized he might appear ungrateful for Morty's concern, so he patted Morty's hand and gave a half smile and then pulled his hand away.

"You're sure. You haven't been in much since… Anyway, if I can help, you know you only have to ask. If you want to talk—"

Morty cut off his words of comfort at the appearance of a new arrival. He directed a look of scorn over Stark's shoulder as Stark felt someone use his left arm as a support to climb on to the stool beside him.

"Hiya, Stark, how ya hangin'?"

"Hello, Roberta, how are you this evening?" Stark knew he would regret asking Roberta Berkowski to tell him how she was, because she would do exactly that, and she did—in a loud voice until Morty finally told her to "shut the fuck up" after which she whispered almost as loudly as she'd been speaking. Stark tuned out most of it, lost in his own thoughts, which centred first on Morty's painful reminder, then drifted to the Harper murder. Roberta's firepower was so heavy, he couldn't help getting hit with snatches of what she was going on about. He got the impression it had something to do with all the "losers" she had to work with, and finally he tuned back in when something dawned on him, and he heard the tail end: "…what a loser. I said, 'get real' and he still goes, 'so, will you go to The Spark with me?' and I go, 'I don't *think* so.' What a loser—"

"Say, Roberta—"

"Mmm."

"You work for an ad agency, don't you?"

"Hello—Earth to Stark," she said with annoyance. "What do you think I've been talking about? The pantyhose campaign, remember? Franko said he wanted to see me in the—"

"Yeah, I'm sorry. I know you work for an ad agency. I was just…anyway, listen, have you heard of Dianne Johnson? She's a marketing consultant, has her own operation—"

"Dianne Johnson—oh, wait a minute—yes, she lives around here somewhere—I think, yeah that *is* her name, but we call her Too Smart, Too Smart Johnson, that's right."

"Why's that?"

"Hmm, well…" Roberta's eyes lit up. Somebody

28

was asking her to impart a piece of gossip, her stock-in-trade, her avocation, her lifeblood. Stark imagined he saw a shimmer of electric current run up her body. She finished off the last of her drink.

"Let me get you another one. What is that?"

"A Bombay Bicycle."

"A what?"

"Never mind. George knows what I drink."

Stark signalled the bartender and pointed to himself and Roberta. They waited in silence. It was obvious Roberta had no intention of starting her tale until she got her drink. He looked at her. Attractive enough, she had long, dark hair, mid-thirties, trim body, but Stark knew she'd be pissed by the end of the night, and she never shut up, except when she was feeling sorry for herself. Then it was a mistake to talk to her at all.

Morty had gone for a pee again. He was fed up. His two "boys" had been visibly unimpressed with his "Detour Ahead," a song that always knocked Stark out, and had left for a rock bar downtown. The two others in his audience appeared to be more interested in chit-chat than listening to Morty.

Sharon, the waitress, six feet tall with a body perfectly proportioned to her height, leaned a breast on Stark's delighted shoulder as she put two glasses on the bar, one an old-fashioned glass containing a familiarly amber Scotch; the other shaped like an hourglass, filled with wedges of orange, lemon and lime and looking more like a fruit salad than a drink. Stark surreptitiously flipped up a corner of the bill. Beside BBC, it said, seven-ninety-five. Some fruit salad. After she'd drawn a healthy draught through the double straws and sucked the maraschino cherry through her pursed lips in an unintentionally suggestive manner, Roberta turned toward Stark with a quizzical "where were we?" look.

"Too Smart," Stark reminded her.

"Right. Well, she's called Too Smart because she used to work for an ad agency, Roy Alcott Paine. We call it Royal Pain because—"

"Roberta. Stick with Too Smart."

"Well, she was with RAP—we also call them rap, but you don't want to hear about that either—"

"No."

She took another sip of her drink. "Well, she thought Royal Pain was 'unimaginative.' That's the word I heard she used. Oh, and the other word was they weren't 'in-off, in-vate, in-oh-vay-tiv, innovative.' I always have problems with that damn word. Too many syllables. Anyway, they weren't *inn*-ovative enough for her. So she went on her own—as a consultant. And she let it be known that the reason Royal Pain wouldn't listen to her was because she was a woman, which is s-o-o-o ridiculous. I mean like, give me a break. They wouldn't listen to her because her ideas were coo-coo. But there's a lot of women in marketing now, so some of them went with her. Actually, she had a good idea, like the consulting thing was a good idea. And really, she's not stupid. I mean they call her Too Smart. She is smart. She just gets carried away. But the good idea was that she went to advertisers and said, 'How do you know that your ad agency's creative ideas are good? You know about making—men's underwear, say, but you don't know about advertising. I do know about advertising—' and she did, because she had a couple of really successful campaigns. Remember that beer commercial with the ferret?"

"Roberta—just—"

"Right. So she was doing really well for a while, and then the Too Smart thing happened again, I mean really happened this time."

"How's that?"

"Well, she got this idea, you know, social responsibility. I mean, it's not really a new thing. A lot of agency people are like that in their personal lives: you know, recycling, bike riding, anti-smoking—can I have one of those Players?"

"I didn't think you—" Roberta was smirking at him. "Yeah, you got me, Roberta. Okay, what—"

"Right. So, like I say, ad people can be really into that stuff, and that's great, you know. Do your own thing, right? But Too Smart had this running-shoe company, Rokflite, for a client. So, you'd think 'running shoes, that's healthy, they'd be socially conscious, right?'"

"I don't think I would, no, Roberta."

"Why not?"

"I had a case—one of their executives was killed. I had to go to Thailand, to one of the factories where they make the shoes." He shook his head. "Pretty rough stuff. Anyway, so Too Smart, as you call her, thought they'd be interested in something socially conscious?"

"Yeah, with kids' shoes, actually. But, you know, Too Smart, but stupid. Let me ask you. You've got—no, you haven't got kids, have you? I mean, were you ever married? Sorry, none of my business, but—"

"Never married. Not really."

"Not really?"

"Never mind. And no kids."

"Oh, okay, well, have you got, like, nephews or something?"

"I don't know much about kids."

"Well, you must have some idea. Let me ask you: Who do you think decides what kind of running shoes a kid's going to buy, like the mother, or the kid?"

"I don't know—the mother, I guess."

"Boy, you should go into business with Too Smart. You'd both lose your shirts. No. The kid, the kid, always the kid. And how does he decide?"

"You tell me."

"He wants what all the other kids are wearing. You get it?"

"Sure, makes sense."

"Exactly. It makes sense, but Too Smart told Rokflite that they'd be a big hit with the mothers, who after all, fork out the dough, if they did a campaign aimed at them, right? So they had some foot doctor with a cutaway of a Rokflite shoe, pointing out—" Roberta put on a deep voice "—'to all you concerned parents' and then he shows all the, what do you call it, orthopaedic advantages of the Rokflite Commander."

"So what happened?"

"Nothing. They still sold the same amount of shoes, because the kids didn't see the commercials, which were run around adult programming. It wouldn't have made any difference, because, like I say, the kids wear what the other kids wear. But the thing is, they tested the commercial's impact, and it was like the lowest rating they'd ever had. Hardly anybody even remembered it, and when they did remember it, they couldn't remember the brand name. So that was the last time Rokflite hired Too Smart. And then she got some other nutso idea about—what was it—oh, yeah, men's briefs. Now—oh never mind, I'm not going to ask you that. The thing is, she convinced the company that since women buy their husbands' underwear and since women have to look at their men in their underwear, why not advertise the underwear to the wives, and also redesign the underwear to make it sexier, okay?"

"Mmm."

"Yeah, right, except it was a complete bomb. They had to repackage the whole line and sell it at a loss to the Buysmart stores. You see you can't force—I mean, men are built in a certain way. You know what I mean. And each guy—well, in the end, men pick underwear that feels good—period."

"So she lost that account, too."

"Right, two big ones. And now she's scrambling to get work, doing little projects for little clients. And not making much money. Anyway, I forgot to ask you, why did you want to know about Too Smart? What's her real name, again?"

"Dianne Johnson."

"Right."

Stark had a sip of Scotch, and Roberta took the opportunity to suck up the rest of her Bombay Bicycle.

"Her husband was killed," Stark said.

"What happened? Oh, my God, you're Homi—"

Stark put his hand up to silence her. "Shh. Keep it down."

Roberta lowered her voice, this time to a truly conspiratorial whisper. "What happened?"

"That's what I'm trying to find out. Want another of those Calcutta Crushes, whatever they are—?"

****

Stark drank so much that Roberta had to help him walk home. They slipped a couple of times on the outside metal stairs to his apartment and the next morning he awoke with a painful bruise on his shin where he'd struck it on the stairs. Roberta had put him in bed, removing his coat and shoes, but leaving him otherwise fully dressed, for which he was thankful.

He'd been drinking himself to sleep most nights for a while, but it still didn't stop the dream, which was always the same: a smiling boy would come toward him with his arms open as if to hug him, and Stark would retreat in terror till he backed into a dark corner. The boy would continue to advance until Stark pulled his gun and shot him, making a large, black hole in the boy's forehead, but the boy would keep coming, still smiling, and Stark would shoot until the gun was empty. The boy would suddenly become Stark's mother, and she would snatch the gun from him and shake him, screaming: "I told you not to play with guns. Now you've killed the dog."

Three months before, Stark had gone into an alley after a punk who had just shot and killed a store clerk during a robbery. Stark heard the call on his radio and spotted the shooter running into the alley. It was not the kind of incident Stark was used to as a Homicide detective, and he had reacted without thinking, without following procedure, without calling for backup. He had leapt out of his car and run into the alley. It was mid-afternoon on a cloudless day, the sun shining brightly intensifying the darkness in the narrow alley. The culprit had wheeled and fired at Stark and Stark had dropped to one knee, raised his gun and fired once just as a twelve-year-old boy, Matthew Hardcastle, had run out the side door of his grandfather's grocery store, where he had been paying his usual after-school visit, in the hope of a chocolate bar. He had a mouthful of the chocolate when Stark's bullet struck him square in the centre of the forehead.

The department hadn't reprimanded Stark immediately, because they couldn't reach him. He had withdrawn into a tiny, dark corner of his mind, and he had spent a week in a psychiatric ward. His superiors wanted to make him take early retirement, and it was only the intervention of a deputy chief, who'd been his first partner on the force, and the recommendation of the force's psychiatrist that kept him on the job. The psychiatrist felt that if Stark didn't go back to work, his mental condition would deteriorate and become irreversible. Stark had been on leave since then.

They'd made him go back to the police college for a remedial course in procedure and safe firearms practice, and he'd had to attend daily sessions with the shrink, which lately had been reduced to once a week. While this helped a little—helped him to come to terms with what had happened—it worked directly against what he really wanted to do: to forget entirely that there had been a shooting, to forget the sweet, chocolate-stained face of that young boy. That, in the end, is why he'd stayed on the force. He'd wanted to quit, but the psychiatrist had warned him that if he did, there would never be a day when he didn't see that face and never a time when he didn't imagine he could hear the boy's plaintive cry. It had helped that he had met Matthew's parents, and they had forgiven him, told him, in fact, there was nothing to forgive, that it had been a terrible accident and that they felt as sorry for him as they did for their son.

The senior ranks who wanted to compel him to retire could find no excuse to insist that he turn in his badge.

The incident had been examined by the Special Investigations Unit. He'd been chastised for being rash, but it had been impossible to find much fault in a policeman's attempting to apprehend an armed criminal who had just shot someone to death. A coroner's inquest had been held quickly, and it had exonerated Stark, the jury's only recommendation being that handguns should be banned. None of this helped Stark, who felt more alone than ever in his lonely life. An only child, whose parents had died when he was in his early twenties, Stark wasn't married, lived alone and had no close friends.

He *had* been married. He'd lied to Roberta when she'd asked him, as he lied to everyone on the subject. The lie had become automatic, because it had all but ceased to be a lie. It wasn't that through some mental black magic he had been able to forget that he had ever been married, but rather that he had put it out of his mind altogether. He *never* thought about it. It had taken him years to accomplish that, but he had succeeded. And it was that *success* that gave him hope that one day he would be able to stop thinking about Matthew Hardcastle—if they would leave him alone.

He would build a shell around it. It would take time. There would be no resolution of the issue. It would lie there in his psyche for all time, as his marriage still lay there, but he would coat it like a piece of grit in an oyster and never have to see it again, as he never had to see the face of his beautiful ex-wife, with whom he'd been so deeply, so completely in love.

She had left him without warning. She had been having an affair for months, even making love in their bed in their little bungalow in East York. She'd left him for a man ten years older than Stark, an actor and playwright who had been directing a play in an amateur theatre group she had joined. She and the playwright lived in Rosedale and had three children.

What Stark wouldn't face, what he would never deal with, was that when he'd applied the solution of shutting out his rejection by his wife, it had ruined his life. It hadn't been enough to cover the marriage with layers of denial; he also had to build a shell around himself, a shell of bitterness, through which he felt nothing. Unfeeling, emotionless, he had become a great investigator, but a lousy person. With his record of success, he should have risen higher in the ranks. He might not have remained a detective if it hadn't been that as a detective-sergeant, he would have had to be responsible for others. He would have had to direct them, listen to them, be concerned for them.

Harry Stark had decided to show the world it couldn't make a fool out of him. He'd convinced himself that he didn't need the world's approbation, or the symbols by which it measured success. But his posing never really worked. Deep down, he saw himself as a failure, and if he'd ever allowed himself to address the subject, he would have recognized that his living alone in a crummy apartment above a Queen Street store was an affectation, part of his self-flagellation.

His bank account was more than healthy. An accountant he'd met as a young cop had taken an interest in him, taken over his financial affairs, invested his money. The accountant had made Stark what most people would have deemed to be reasonably well-off, if not quite wealthy. And yet if Stark had said he had no idea how much money he had, he would have been telling the truth. And that was an affectation, too.

But the terrible shooting of that boy had cracked the shell of uncaring, which was a good deal thinner than he'd realized, and now he had the same dream almost every night, and sometimes when a sudden movement caught the corner of his eye, he would see the boy emerge from the doorway again. And he would start to shake. It had been the first time he'd fired his gun on duty and he swore to God it would be the last.

The psychiatrist had elicited from him that his mother's appearance in the dream stemmed from a childhood incident, an incident in which he'd hit the neighbour's dog with a ballbearing fired from a slingshot fashioned out of a wire coat hanger and a wide elastic band that he'd bought in a hobby shop. With the neighbour woman standing in the Starks' front hall, his mother had pulled his pants down, and spanked him.

Stark had been back on the job a week before the Harper killing. His inspector, who intended to push him out of the Homicide Unit, wouldn't have wanted him on the case, but a detective-sergeant who liked Stark had been on duty when the call came in and deliberately phoned him at home.

On the morning after Roberta had brought him home, Stark's first thought was whether she had spent the night in the apartment. The last thing he wanted was to face Roberta Berkowski over his morning Scotch and coffee. He tiptoed through the apartment until he determined she wasn't there. Then he bent over the kitchen sink and drank as much water as he could as it ran from the tap. Bending over was a mistake. When he stood up, his head started to pound and his legs went rubbery. After a moment, he shook it off, made the coffee and poured the Scotch. He sat at the kitchen table, gulped the Scotch in one before he could change his mind, and shook his jowls like a bloodhound. Sipping the creamy coffee, he began to review the murder he had to solve.

Motive? The missing wallet suggested it could have been robbery. But nothing else was taken. The boot print suggested that somebody came to the apartment in the late afternoon, or at least sometime after it had snowed. On the other hand, the boot print could have nothing to do with the killing at all. Whoever smacked Harper must have known him. The floors are too creaky in the apartment for him not to have heard someone coming up behind him. He wouldn't have just sat there until he got whacked unless he had known the person making the noise.

So burglary is unlikely. And yet the wallet *is* missing, so it could have been a burglary gone wrong. The burglar, maybe a kid, carrying whatever to protect himself, or maybe just picking up something in the apartment. But where is it? Stark made a mental note to ask the wife whether anything is missing. But why would the assailant take the weapon with him? Panic, Stark supposed.

The wife was due to return. The husband thinks it's her. "Is that you dear?" he says, and continues at the computer, absorbed in his work. The culprit, having been discovered, panics, grabs something and smacks the guy on the head, not intending to kill him. Then what? Before he gets a chance to leave or to ransack the place, or whatever, the wife actually does come in. The culprit closes the door to the workroom, maybe hides behind it.

He hears her go into the kitchen, sneaks out, maybe intending to smack her, too, but she doesn't turn around, and he sees the closet, with the bolt locks, pulls on the balaclava. She turns, which is when she sees the balaclava, and he grabs her and shoves her into the closet, the pantry, or whatever it is, and then he runs out the front door, and all he's got is the guy's wallet. "Could be—but I don't think so."

****

The Centre of Forensic Science wasn't very helpful. As the detective in charge of the case, Stark attended the autopsy. Cause of death, blow from the proverbial blunt object—something at least 15 centimetres wide, the extent of the skull area that had been damaged; too wide for a baseball bat; something heavy; probably something longish that would be aided in the swing by centrifugal force. Most likely, the blow had been delivered by a man, although with the right length, heft and shape of weapon, a woman could have done it. Time of death, between four and six hours before the body was examined, so before five o'clock.

Chapter Four

Jennifer Johnson had an apartment in the rear of the top floor of a three-storey converted and yuppified house in Cabbagetown, divided into six units. A similar building on the left was boarded up and colourfully splashed with mainly incomprehensible graffiti, and Stark recognized it as the site of a crack dealer's murder two years earlier. The matching building on the right was an unyuppified rooming house, divided into sixteen units. A wraith-like man of indeterminate age sat shivering in a short denim jacket on the front steps, drinking from a bottle in a brown paper bag. Someone was curled up asleep on the stoop.

In the middle of the highly polished oak door of the house where Johnson lived, there was a massive, fluted, round brass knob. Above the door was a video camera. To the right of the door was a double row of glass-covered nameplates, rimmed in gleaming brass, each with a last name and first initial, and each with a black button beside it. Stark pressed the button opposite "J. Johnson." He waited almost thirty seconds before a high-pitched, but husky, voice unpleasantly said: "Step back where I can see you." He complied with the order and looked up at the camera. He opened his mouth to introduce himself, but before he could speak, the voice said, "Come in," and he heard a buzzer as the door was unlocked and then opened by an electric motor.

He stepped into a black-and-white tiled vestibule and faced another door, this one with a thick, bevelled glass insert. He tried that door, but it wouldn't open. The voice spoke again, from a speaker in the vestibule. "It won't open until the outside door is closed." The outside door was being electrically swung shut. As soon as it had clicked closed, he heard the lock of the inside door pop open. Through that, he entered a long hallway, which had a Persian carpet runner flanked by varnished hardwood flooring. A huge crystal chandelier sparkled overhead. A flight of stairs ran up parallel to the hallway with matching runner and hardwood. He stood for an instant and listened to the steady drip of utter silence. Not a single stair creaked as he climbed to the third floor.

Jennifer Johnson was waiting outside her door. Automatically Stark took his badge out, but before he could introduce himself, she said, more like an order than a request, "Take it easy on her. She's badly shaken up. It wouldn't take much for her to snap."

"Stark—" he said, with no acknowledgement of her instructions. "—Detective Harry Stark."

"I know who you are. The woman cop told me."

"Can we go in?"

She held the door open. She was tall and thin, shapeless, in baggy jeans and a yellow plaid shirt. Long, straight hair in a pony tail. No makeup, which made her very young face younger. Stark didn't know whether she was the older or the younger of the sisters.

"Cold day," he said as he passed her.

"Mmm," she said without smiling.

The floor was thickly carpeted in a champagne colour. Obviously installed by the owners of the building, it was the only item you could call decor in the place. The rest, starkly utilitarian, consisted of one large room, a door at one corner to the bathroom, a windowed door at the opposite corner to the fire escape, and an open door in the middle to a walk-in closet where Stark could see a mountain bike, a jumble of sports equipment, a stack of cardboard cartons, a pile of dirty clothes and a few clean ones hanging. The walls were bare eggshell white, trimmed in lightly stained oak. Not a single painting hung, no posters. In the work area, there was a Milk Marketing Board calendar with an illustration of a pasta dish.

The work area itself was pristine. In addition to a large-screen Mac computer, there was a scanner and a variety of other computer-related and office equipment and a drafting board. The windows were covered with closed venetian blinds, no curtains.

The kitchen area, separated by an L-shaped counter, was festooned with dirty pots and dishes. There was a large wok on the stove, half-filled with food from some previous meal. On one wall, there was a small rack of bookshelves stacked on bricks, which reminded Stark of his university days.

A T-shirt and a sweat sock were draped over one corner. The room was large enough that Stark had to look around to find Dianne Johnson. She was behind the dinette set, sitting in the corner of a Danish modern couch, the only other piece of furniture in the room. The couch was upholstered in grey, with a large brown stain at one end and one leg that had been badly chewed by some puppy.

Dianne Johnson looked as if she might have been chewed by the same puppy. The curl in her hair had lost its spring and sat on her head like a rain-ravaged bird's nest. She was wearing an outsized, purple University of Western Ontario sweatshirt. She was as far into the corner of the couch as she could get, bolt upright and staring into space.

Stark took a deep breath. "I'm sorry, Mrs—*Ms* Johnson—" He gave an almost idiotic half smile and glanced awkwardly at the sister, looking for approval of his choice of honorific. He was about a decade behind culturally. Jennifer Johnson hadn't even noticed Stark's clumsy effort. She was looking at Dianne with an expression of real concern.

"I won't take much of your time," Stark said. "I just want to go over one or two things—you know, very briefly. Really, really briefly." He waited for some acknowledgement, but there was no response. Finally, he sat on one of the dinette chairs and took a deep breath. "Well," he said at last, "last night, you told the other officers that you got home about eight-forty-five?" No response. He sighed. "Look, Ms Johnson. I-I know this is painful for you, but—"

"Yes," she said. Her voice was flat, drained of emotion, numb.

"Right. And you said you put your suitcase away— by the way, where were you arriving from? You'd been away?"

"Ottawa—I was visiting a friend—from school."

"Right. And you—so you came into the house, and you put your suitcase in the bedroom—the office door was closed. Was that usual? Did your husband—would he have closed the door when he was alone in the apartment?"

She glanced at Stark quickly, then looked straight ahead again. "He likes to play music when he works—"

44

Stark noticed her use of the present tense. "—old rock and roll records. He has a collection of 45 rpm discs—"

"I noticed the player there, the little square box with the wide spindle. I used to have one—a long time ago." Stark shook his head at the realization that a lot of time, a lot of life, had passed since then.

"They were his father's, the player, too. He plays—played the records loud. With the door open, you can hear downstairs. The landlord—he lives there—complained."

"So he always closed the door. I mean, your husband closed the door, not the landlord."

"Yes."

"You went into the kitchen?"

"Yes. I was going to make him a coffee. He likes—" She shook her head, touched her forehead with the fingers of one hand. The sister went and sat beside her, putting an arm around her shoulders. Dianne Johnson took a deep breath and let it out. "I started to make the coffee, and then somebody grabbed me—from behind. He had gloves on. He put a hand over my mouth. He was strong. He dragged me—over to the pantry, and pushed me in. And then he locked the door with the key, and bolted it."

"You didn't scream or shout, bang on the door after he closed it? Tried to open it?"

"Yes, I did. I shouted—I shouted till I was hoarse. And then I—then I listened, and I couldn't hear anything. I tried to hear. I listened for Chris. I think I called out his name—I did. I know I called his name. And then I listened—and—I started to shiver. I was—it was—"

"I understand. You were in there for a couple of hours. I must have been very rough not knowing—is

45

there a light in there?"

"Yes."

"Uh-huh. okay, so after a while, when you didn't hear anything, any sound, any voices from the apartment, I wonder why—or maybe you did—why you didn't try to jimmy the door open?"

"Jesus," Jennifer Johnson said, glaring at Stark.

"That's a very heavy door," Dianne said. "Believe me, I shook it and smashed myself against it and—I kicked it. We don't have any crowbars or anything like that in there. It's a pantry. I looked for something. I *did* look for something. You don't think I just sat there, not knowing whether my husband needed help. I kept praying that he wasn't there, that he'd gone out to the store before the burglar broke in, or that he was tied up. I never thought—I never allowed myself to think—"

"Yes, of course. So, now, when he came up behind you—You know, I noticed the floor creaks rather loudly in a couple of spots—and it appears he was wearing boots. You didn't hear him?"

She shook her head and closed her eyes. "I thought..." She sighed. "I thought it was my husband. I thought he was going to—even when the—arm went around me, I thought it was Chris giving me a hug. You see, we—"

"You what?"

"Nothing. I was just thinking of—something else."

Stark shrugged.

"Okay. So, the only thing the assailant took was your husband's wallet?"

"As far as I could see. I didn't look thoroughly. One of the policeman said Chris's gold watch with the nugget watch fob was still there. One of the companies he works for gave it to him. It's very valuable."

"Tell me, did your husband carry his wallet in his *back* pocket?"

"Yes."

"So, if he was sitting—and he was, of course—in the office chair, anyone coming into the room, would have been able to see the wallet, because the chair is open at the back, right? Open at the bottom, with a back support higher up."

"I guess so. Yeah, it's like that."

"Right. In your area, there are very few break-ins. You know, I mean, there are kids, taking VCRs, radios, things they can sell on the street. So, it's a bit unusual, this. Your husband didn't have any enemies—no one who might—"

Her eyes gaped in an expression that mixed horror and anger.

"No!" she shouted.

Jennifer Johnson glared at Stark.

"Can't you figure it out? It seems so obvious to me. Dianne must have got there just after the guy. And then when she started to yell, he panicked, and took off down the back stairs, the way he'd come in. He didn't get a chance to take anything else. It's as simple as that. Why are you complicating things?"

"You're probably right." Stark smiled and nodded patronizingly. "Okay, all right, one other thing. Can you tell me—what was in your husband's wallet? Driver's licence—?"

"Yes, of course."

"Credit cards?"

She nodded

"Cash? Would he have been carrying a lot of cash?"

"He never had any money. A few dollars. If he wanted money, he'd ask me."

"Okay. Well—yeah, right." Stark nodded and closed his notebook. "I guess that's it then." He put the notebook in his jacket pocket and stood up. Then he raised a finger as if he'd just remembered something. "You know, there were a lot of dishes, glasses mostly, and empty wine bottles in the kitchen. Would your husband have been entertaining when you were away?"

"Yes. He was going to have some friends over. Friends of his—geologists—I can't—well, frankly, they're boring. All they talk about is rocks. So he was— he was going to have them over while I was away."

"I see. Well, do you think you could give me a list of the names—of the people he would have had over?"

"Why? Why would you want that?"

Stark made a dismissive gesture.

"Well, they might have seen somebody hanging around the neighbourhood. You never know," he said with a synthetic smile.

"I know who they are," Jennifer said. She went to the work area, wrote on a pad, and tore off the top sheet. "Here, these are all the people who would have been there. Maybe not all of them, but some would have been there." She pointed to a line she had written beneath the list of names, which read, "Phone numbers in address book on phone table in apartment." Stark nodded. Jennifer didn't want her sister to be bothered by the fact that he was going to be prowling around her apartment.

Chapter Five

Homer Wingate and Joyce Lee were sitting in the back corner booth at Holtzman's when Stark came in. They were in an animated discussion about something, and didn't notice Stark. He got close enough to hear what they were saying and stopped.

"The trouble with you is, you don't want to be a woman. You resent it."

"You arrogant, chauvinist pig. What the hell gives you the right—no, not you alone—you, you, *males*—the right to decide what a woman should and shouldn't be like? I'm a woman, asshole, and whatever I do, I do as a woman. Whatever I do and say is what a woman does or says. Get it, dickhead?"

"Gentlemen—uh, people, please, is this the image of the Metropolitan Toronto Police Service we want to present to the public? The language. Really, Constable Lee. I'm surprised at you."

"Sorry, Sarge."

"You should be. And you have to say 'male chauvinist.' The word 'chauvinist' alone means a jingoistic patriot."

"Were you an English major, Sarge?" Lee asked.

Stark chuckled.

"No—I just have this annoying habit of correcting people's grammar. It's rude and tiresome. Sorry." He shrugged.

"That's all right. You did go to university, though, didn't you? What did you take?"

"Sociology, actually." Stark slipped into the booth beside Lee, his thigh touching hers for an instant until she quickly shifted over. "I didn't graduate. Sort of washed out on a tide of draft beer. But the sociology led to my becoming a cop—reading things like *Street Corner Society*. I realized that standing back and observing these little pricks objectively, as if they were some sort of lost tribe, didn't make much sense. I figured they shouldn't be hanging around on street corners, denying them to hard-working, honest, ordinary human beings. So, I got me a nightstick and I went out and cracked a few heads. It was my first real-life learning experience. And you know what I found out?"

"What's that?" Wingate asked.

"It didn't work. I cleaned up my street corners, all right, but the punks just moved somewhere else. Shifting a problem isn't solving it. But then I also realized that solving society's problems *isn't* my job. Solving crimes? Yeah, that's my job. At least, I *like* solving crimes. Solving people's problems—the hell with it."

"Sounds a bit—you know, cynical, Sarge, if you don't mind me saying it?"

"'My' saying it."

"Sorry?"

"Never mind. Have you two been asking around about the Harper killing?"

"Yeah," Wingate looked at Lee. "We did—a little. We're not really supposed to, but the Division dicks don't seem to be doing much. I don't know if I should be saying this, Sarge, but I don't think they like you."

Stark laughed.

"So, what'd you find out?"

"Well—really, nothing. I mean, we interviewed a couple of the neighbours who weren't home the night of the crime. You know: 'Did you see anything unusual?' That sort of thing. And nothing. And we remembered hearing you ask Jim Cory if he'd asked the landlord what he heard. So we asked the landlord. And he said he heard nothing."

"Nothing?"

Lee said, "Well, he heard nothing that sounded like a struggle, or any sort of thump or scraping, or anything like that. He heard no noise that he especially remembered."

"No noise." Stark looked thoughtful. "I spoke with the wife."

"Was she helpful?"

"Not much. The one thing I'm pretty sure of is, whoever killed him knew him."

"How do you figure that?" Wingate asked eagerly. "Because he was wearing the balaclava so he wouldn't be recognized by the wife? No, that doesn't make sense. Why wouldn't he just kill her, too? Come to think of it, why *didn't* he kill her? Unless he was wearing the balaclava for psychological reasons—because, if he knew them—"

Stark put his hand up to silence the young constable.

"He had to know Harper because of the way in which Harper was killed. That's an old house. The floor in there creaks badly. Even without that, there's no way you could sneak up on somebody in that house without making some sort of noise that Harper would hear and turn around and then jump up and try to fend off his attacker. Instead, he keeps sitting there, working at something on the computer, and, bingo, he's bopped on the back of the head. With what? Well, that's a big question mark. No sign of a weapon. I got Cory and Weems seconded to do a thorough search of the area this morning, after the uniforms had looked last night, and they found nothing."

Lee gave a dry laugh.

"We saw the search. Cory and Weems sat in the doughnut shop, drinking coffee. They had six uniforms checking every garbage can and under every porch in a two-block radius."

Stark shook his head.

"Well, anyway, they didn't find anything. Doesn't mean it's not around somewhere. Be hard to hide, though, the way it's described by forensic. Got to be six or seven inches wide at least. Not something you could drop through a sewer grate. Unless he took it with him."

"Sarge, about you saying Harper had to know the person—"

"'Your saying'."

"What?"

"Never mind. What about it?"

"Well, the landlord said he might not have heard anything because Harper kept the office door closed because he used to listen to loud music I mean, that could—"

Stark sighed, shook his head, and then nodded.

"Yes, it's possible. It's just too neat. It's like he's sitting there as a perfect target." He swept his hand in imitation of a blow. "Bang, right on the back of the head." He swung the hand downward. "And bop, his head goes straight down, his face right on the keyboard of the computer. You'd think—I would think—that you'd sense somebody in the room, that you'd turn, even a little bit, to one side or the other, that the odds are you'd do that—unless you *knew*—unless you were comfortable with and had no reason to fear the person who was in the room with you."

****

The apartment was full of smells. Musty, the air having been still since the night of the killing, Sunday. Now it was the middle of Tuesday morning. It smelled also of coffee and spices and cleanser and furniture polish. Stark noticed the smells particularly because his own apartment was so redolent of Gauloises cigarettes, Dunhill pipe tobacco and Cuban cigars that any other odour was practically undetectable. Maybe, you might smell dirty socks, but you'd certainly never smell cleanser or furniture polish.

He was poking into things, opening drawers, looking under socks and underwear, finding meaningless bits of paper, receipts, old birthday and anniversary cards, the scraps of two lives, a photograph of the couple, which he put in his jacket pocket. The gold watch and nugget fob were there, as they'd said. No sign of a burglar's rough search. He went into the kitchen. If she'd been making him a coffee—some indication. There were two cups on the table. He remembered the wife and the sister sitting there. The sister must have made coffee. There was the clutter from the husband's get-together. Dishes with cake crumbs and the hardened residue of chocolate ice cream; espresso demitasses and regular coffee cups and various glasses: beer steins, a brandy snifter, liqueur glasses, old-fashioned glasses; a silver wine bucket with a dead bottle turned top down and draped with an empty polyethylene ice bag; three empty

Heineken bottles.

The key was in the lock of the pantry door. There were two massive slide bolts. The door was unlocked; the bolts were slid back. He looked into the pantry. More smells—onion skins and herbs. The pantry was lined with shelves, filled with recycled jars holding a variety of cooking ingredients. A pile of brown paper bags, neatly folded, stood at one end, a half-dozen string shopping bags stacked on top of the paper ones. There was a recycling box on the floor, stacked with newspapers—the *Globe and Mail*, the *Northern Miner*. Four papers down, he stopped, momentarily surprised to see his own face grinning back at him. The Beaches paper had done an article about him. He'd had to get departmental permission. They'd jumped at the idea, community policing being the big thing these days. He'd only done it because the editor had helped him with a case, sat on some information that, by itself, wouldn't have added much to a story, but would have sent a suspect into hiding. Stark had had to promise that he'd let the guy do a story on him—if he could get permission, which he was counting on not getting, but did. He thought his grin was as inane as the headline, "Super sleuth snoops in the Beaches." In mumbling embarrassment, he covered it quickly with the other papers.

He went into the office, ducking under the crime-scene yellow tape, as he'd done when he entered the apartment before. In contrast with the disarray in the kitchen, this room was a picture of neatness. He thought of his desk at home—a computer surrounded by a scrap heap of paper and books and file trays and overflowing ashtrays and coffee cups lined with hardened residue.

Here, there was not a single scrap of paper on any work surface.

Here, except for the plaques and posters and maps on the walls that helped define the two work areas and a multicoloured display of mineral-laden rocks on a square of black velvet, there was nothing that didn't directly relate to the serious activities that took place—that *had* taken place—in this room. He looked cursorily through the two filing cabinets—in hers he found nothing that struck him as being of interest. And, similarly, in Harper's until he opened the lowest of the three drawers, one hanging file was slightly raised from the others. It was labelled *X-King*, and it was empty.

He turned on Harper's computer, typed "win" at the C prompt and fired up Windows. The array of icons was considerably greater than on his own computer, most of these for programs he didn't recognize. He double clicked on Word and in a fraction of the time it took to load the program on his own machine, a blank document screen appeared. He clicked on file, and at the bottom of the display were the names of the last four files that had been opened. Three of them had long pathnames that looked technical, but the top one, the most recent, was labelled C:\CORR\DILET.DOC. He double clicked on that and a letter flashed onto the screen. It was addressed, "My Dear Chris." Stark skimmed the letter.

"Son of a bitch," he said, and pulled out his pack of Gauloises. He turned on the laser printer, clicked on the print icon and went into the kitchen to look for some instant coffee. "Should have known," he muttered when his search for coffee proved fruitless. He looked at the massive espresso machine and shook his head. There was a drip coffee maker on the counter, but in the end, after rifling through an assortment of herbal teas, he managed only to find a small package of Earl Grey. He dropped a bag in a mug, boiled the kettle and poured the water—on the boil, as his mother had taught him—over the tea bag. He pressed the bag with a teaspoon to hurry the process, fished out the bag and added a drop of milk. "Sorry, Mom," he said, with a glance skyward. She'd have been annoyed that he hadn't put the milk in first, but "You can't do that when you're making it in a cup, dear."

He took a sip from the brimming mug, spilling some on the kitchen floor, returned to the office, took the letter from the printer, and read it slowly.

"Since you're reading this, I must have spoken to you on the phone and told you to look for it in the correspondence file. If you've found it accidentally by yourself, it doesn't matter. I wanted to put this in writing so you would know how serious I am. What I'm going to say is very simple: I'LL NEVER LET YOU LEAVE ME. I know what you've been doing and what you plan to do, but I realize that I couldn't stand that. I know now the last three years have been a mistake. It's going to end. We're both going to make big changes. You WILL stop thinking of nothing but rocks. YOU WILL include me in your life. I know now it's the only way for both of us. If you can get so emotional, so angry about X-King, you can save some of that emotion for me. I've been wrong. I took the wrong course in this thing, and now I'm going to change EVERYTHING. Chris. I mean this. I WILL NOT LET YOU LEAVE ME. I WILL NOT BE TOSSED ASIDE ON SOME SLAG HEAP. I WOULD SOONER KILL YOU AND THEN KILL MYSELF."

He re-read "I WOULD SOONER KILL YOU,"

grunted and shook his head. "What the hell." He went back to the computer and opened the file manager. He opened every directory. Many of the file names looked familiar. He pulled open the top drawer on the "his" filing cabinet. There they were. Most of the labels on the hanging files corresponded with file names in the computer. He tried a few more at random, and found a matching computer file for each, but there was no X-King. He did a search on "X-King" and found nothing. From his jacket pocket, he pulled out a small phone directory, and looked up the number for Charlie Hayden, who was the chief investigator with the surveillance department of the Ontario Securities Commission.

"Hayden. This is not voice mail; this is Hayden, himself, in the all-too-ample flesh. What, dear caller, can I do for you today?" Hayden's English-major's voice always reminded Stark of oiled ball-bearings.

"Charlie, it's Harry Stark."

"Harry, my boy, how are you? I haven't seen you in a dog's age. We must get together for a snifter. What can I do for you?"

"Charlie, have you ever heard of something called X-King? It would be in the mining field, I think."

"X-King, X-King. No, I'm sorry, Harry, that's a new one on me. I can ask around if you like, and get back to you. In fact, why don't I do that and we'll combine a little pleasure with business. Come and see me tomorrow and we'll have lunch. Make it about one-thirty."

"I'll do that. In the meantime, find out what you can about Chris Harper."

"Are you on that case? Terrible thing, absolutely terrible. He was a genius, you know. He'll be missed terribly in the mining industry. Of course, I know a great deal about him *now*. Is there anything specific?"

"No. Just see what he was involved in recently, how his business was doing, that sort of thing."

"Very good, sir. I certainly will do that. Until tomorrow."

"Right, see you," Stark said, and hung up.

He finished his tea, shut down the computer, and for the next hour, opened every file in both filing cabinets and poked into every crack and crevice in the apartment, looking for anything that said "X-King." No luck.

He got ready to leave, washing his cup and the saucer he'd used as an ashtray. Just before he left, he remembered the sister's note. He found the phone directory, looked up the names she had given him, and copied down the addresses and numbers.

At the door, he took the keys out of his pocket to make sure he had them, and paid attention for the first time to the fact that there were two other keys on the chain. Not house keys; one was more like the key to a filing cabinet. He tried it on the two cabinets in the office, but it didn't fit. The other key was slightly larger, but there appeared to be no lock in the apartment it would have opened. He put the keys away, and left.

Outside, he stood in the driveway for a moment, staring at the building as if it could tell him something. Then, absently, he strolled to the back of the house. The footprint was still clearly visible. There'd been no new snowfall. The print wasn't as distinct as it had been on the day of the murder. The temperature had risen dramatically as a small warm front passed through, and the streets had become coated with the dreaded Toronto slush.

There was no car in the driveway. The sister could

have taken it, of course. He tried the garage door. Locked. He pulled the keys out of his pocket, and tried the larger one of the strange pair in the garage lock. It opened. The Honda was inside and unlocked. He looked in the glove compartment, under the seats, popped the trunk—nothing. You could have eaten off the floor of the thing.

He looked around the garage. At the rear he saw a large metal cupboard. He went to it quickly. The smaller key opened it. It was full of camping gear and Harper's geology equipment, little pointed axes and leather boxes of instruments. On the bottom shelf of the cabinet, there was a duffel bag. One boot sat on top of the bag. He put the boot aside and rummaged through the bag. Camping gear. He pulled the string closed on the bag and put the boot back on top of it. Then he picked the boot up and looked at it, turned it over, walked out of the garage with it and laid it down, sole up, beside the footprint in the snow. A perfect match.

Chapter Six

That night at Carbo's, Monty was acting more petulant than usual. Finally, he opened up to Stark. "It's that fucking Greek, Harold. Last night, there was couple in here from Newmarket, or some Godforsaken suburban wasteland. First, they asked me to play 'New York, New York.' You know I never play that turkey, and then they asked me to play 'Feelings.' Can you imagine, fucking 'Feelings.' Christ, if they'd asked for 'Spanish Eyes' I'd have strangled both of them with my bare hands. You'd be arresting *me* for murder. Anyway, I told them as politely as possible that I didn't play that sort of *thing*.

"Ulysses heard the whole thing. I mean, the couple didn't complain, and I was diplomatic, practically apologetic, *self-deprecating*, you could say. So much so, I think they figured I probably didn't know *how* to play the fucking pieces. But then Ulysses comes on with 'The customer is always right.' Well, not quite, but he did say something ridiculously infantile, like 'Don't forget, Morty, *they* pay your salary. *They* are your employers.' Asshole. So I said, 'What you're saying is that if somebody asks for 'You Picked a Fine Time to Leave me, Lucille,' I'm supposed to belt it out like Garth Brooks or whoever sang the thing, is that it?' Then the little Greek prick—and by the way, he has—" Stark rolled his eyes. "—he gets all shirty and says, 'Just play the god-damned requests.' and stomps off. What an asshole. God, what I'm reduced to—me, in this dead-end dump. You know, I sang with Percy Faith and—"

"Yes, I know, Morty, Glen Gray."

"You speak as if you disbelieve me. I'm sorry, am I boring you?" Morty said with self-indulgent angst.

"No, Morty. Forget it—you're a great talent. How many times have I told you, you run the best god-damned piano bar in the whole world? And I've heard some greats, Wally Aspell in Montreal, Paul Drake and that guy with the big moustache used to play in the old Hyatt—before that, he played in Johnny's Piano Bar in Montreal, what was his name—"

"Yes, yes, you've been around, big boy. Never mind me, I'm just—" Morty sighed. "All right, what can I play for you?"

A woman's voice answered, "'Here's That Rainy Day.'" Stark's head spun around. Leaning on the back of the bar stool beside his was Carol Weems. She wasn't dressed for work. She was wearing a long, clingy, black-knit outfit. Her hair was permed and held up with a large silver clip in the back. Her face was intensively, but attractively, made up—hunting gear, Stark thought, and he smiled.

Morty went into unctuous mode. "My, what great musical taste, and in one so young and lovely. It's so rare these days. Did you know that that number is Harold's favourite? This is Harold, by the way, or perhaps you—"

"We know each other," Stark said.

"Yes, I'll bet you do. Well, let me entertain you, as Rosalind Russell would say, or was it Natalie Wood?"

Morty ran through 'Here's That Rainy Day' in three styles, three tempos, changing key for the last go-round, improvising, adding rich arpeggios, giving the 'funny' at the start of the last line six syllables, Mel Tormé style. It was such an impressive effort that a couple at the bar joined Stark and Weems in applause, and then came over and sat on the opposite side of the piano bar. Morty was inspired and outdid himself with each succeeding number, playing now for the new arrivals and allowing Stark and Weems to talk.

As it was, they didn't talk much. Weems pressed her knee into Stark's thigh as soon as she sat down, refused to let him discuss the Harper case, and spent most of the time staring at him and saying "Uh huh," to whatever he said. It took him a while to realize that chit-chat wasn't necessary. Finally, he slid off his stool, extended an arm toward the door and said, "Shall we?" and they left with a smile and a wave to Morty, who nodded and winked.

This time, Stark persuaded himself she wasn't faking with her routine. In fact, he got right into the spirit of the thing, himself, and the two of them bayed at the moon like a couple of hound dogs.

She didn't stay the night. In fact, after they'd had a coffee, she excused herself, saying that she had an early shift the next day.

Stark was delighted. He got dressed, chanting, Professor Higgins' "Why Can't a Woman Be More Like a Man", and thinking that he might have found one who was. He was doubly delighted because it was still an hour-and-a-half till closing, and he was able to go back to Carbo's, have a couple of large brandies—in the hope it would put him to sleep without the dream—and sing with Morty, whose only comment on Stark's rapid return was that he must be losing it if that was all he could handle.

****

The next day, Stark paid a visit to Homicide. Marilyn, the unit's secretary, had called him three times, each call more frantic than the last. The detective-sergeant who'd assigned Stark to the case was screaming for a report on the Harper killing. The inspector heard the bitching and vowed that as soon as the case was over, he was going to put Stark on permanent desk duty. The brandies hadn't put Stark to sleep, so he'd sat at his computer and written a report until his eyelids had drooped closed and his chin had slumped on to his chest.

He was going to send the report to the detective sergeant by modem, but when he'd reread it in the morning, he'd thought he'd said both too much and not enough in it, and had decided to give it orally. But when he'd arrived at headquarters, he'd found the DS was out. In the end, he left the written report on the sergeant's desk, gave Marilyn a hug and made his escape.

There was no coffee shop in the area that would let him smoke his Gauloises, so he sat on a bench in front of city hall and watched the skaters spin and weave over the pond. It was warm in the sun, and he sat and smoked, blowing great billows of smoke and condensed breath that wafted over the figures of the skaters, long-limbed girls in little skirts and leotards; mothers in down-filled coats and leggings, towing shaky-legged tots; teenagers, whose machismo demanded they be bareheaded and wear short, thin jackets; businessmen in long overcoats, taking a break with a little brisk exercise, something Stark would never have done.

Stark sat and thought about Dianne Johnson. She bothered him. Her note bothered him. He was bothered that she was in the apartment right after the murder and could easily have been there before the murder. And yet she was so neatly put out of the picture by being locked in the pantry. She couldn't have locked the door herself. She couldn't have got rid of the weapon. What weapon? What the hell was the weapon? And the boot, the boot in the garage, an exact match to the print in the snow. That didn't seem to make any sense at all. It appeared to have been Harper's boot, and yet how—why would he wear the boot going into the apartment and then come back down the stairs and leave the boot in the garage? And why was just the one boot left on top of the duffel bag?

What Roberta had said about Johnson bothered him, too. She'd called her "Too Smart," as in "too smart for her own good." She was a failure. Stark, an expert on failure, knew it could make you bitter and resentful. He'd seen it make people kill before.

Johnson's husband was a great success. When Stark was a young man, a husband's success was usually enough for a wife, but this was a different time. If Harper planned to leave her, to dump her—. What if she'd had an accomplice? What if she had a boyfriend, who'd worn the balaclava in case he'd been spotted coming and going? What if the boyfriend had taken the wallet to make it look like a botched burglary. Johnson, after all, had pointed out that the wallet was missing.

Chapter Seven

Stark began to run down the list of attendees at the victim's soirée. The first, William Watson, lived in Don Mills. The bungalow had been ultramodern when it was built in the fifties, when fashion mandated that every stick of furniture be Danish. The low-angled roof covered a carport sheltering an aging car.

Stark had risen at seven and called all the names on the list, asking each whether he or she wanted to be interviewed at home or at the office. They had all chosen home, except Christine Harvey, who had asked him to meet her for lunch the next day. He had made appointments to see each of them but Philip Symchuk, who was out of the country and wouldn't be back for at least a week, according to his secretary.

He had also tried to arrange an interview with Harper's partner, Shane Bishop. The answering service supervisor gave him Bishop's home number after Stark had satisfied her that he was a policeman, but the woman who'd answered Bishop's phone—she had a funny little, artificial-sounding voice and identified herself as his sister—said the news of Harper's murder had devastated her brother, and that he was in bed under heavy sedation, and she had asked whether Stark could wait till Friday, to which he had agreed.

****

William Watson was short and round. Every part of

him seemed round, as if he had been assembled from spheres of varying size, like a snowman. He had a ratty fringe of a beard—grown in a futile attempt to add some maturity to his boyish face—succeeding only in making him look ridiculous. Extremely nervous, he had an annoying habit of wringing his hands. He was so jumpy it ran through Stark's mind that shouting at him might make him pee like a puppy. His reaction to Stark's questions magnified the puppy image—he yipped out the first couple of words, startled.

"It's a terrible thing, horrible," Watson said, knotting his hands in a physical display of his feeling of horror.

"Mmm." Stark nodded. "Mr Watson, during your evening with Mr Harper, did he appear, say, distracted, nervous? Did he say anything that might have suggested he felt he was in any danger, for instance, or perhaps that he was disturbed about something, worried about something?"

Watson twitched. "No, not at all. He seemed perfectly relaxed. We all had a good time, chatting about this and that, you know—we all know each other quite well, you see."

"There were no arguments throughout the evening, no sharp words?"

"Oh no," he yelped. "Disagreements, yes, but over technical things, interpretations of data, geological matters, you understand? Do you know anything about geology, Mr Stark?"

"No, no I don't."

"Ooo," he squealed and Stark looked up sharply. "There was—something, but until now—well, it seemed inconsequential—I'd forgotten all about it."

"What's that?"

"It was that he said—somebody asked him how things were going in his business, and he said—he paused and said something like, 'Everything's great, except I've got a small problem that I have to take care of before it becomes a big problem.' And then somebody said, 'What's that?' and he said, 'Oh, it's nothing, a minor glitch, not worth discussing,' and then he changed the subject, and that was it. He'd had quite a bit of wine by that time. In the end, he passed out on the couch—well, I should say, fell asleep, really."

"A minor glitch, not worth discussing?"

"That's right."

"He didn't mention a person who was part of the problem, didn't say a name?"

"Nooo. Not that I—no, I'm sure he didn't. He really—I'm sure it was of no consequence. You know how people get when they've had a few too many."

"And yet you remembered it."

"Well, I wouldn't have if you hadn't asked me and made me think—about every, you know, detail. That's all."

"Did you know Harper's wife—Dianne Johnson?"

"Oh, yes, of course, but we didn't—she wasn't usually with Chris whenever we got together. It's understandable. We can be incredibly boring, you know, if you're not a geologist—a rockhead." He giggled.

"Harper and his wife, do you know whether they were having any problems?"

"Financial problems? Well, she's been having trouble with her business. Chris was a bit concerned about it."

"He spoke about it?"

"Well—in the past. Not the night of the party."

"Actually, I didn't mean financial problems. I meant—marital problems Were he and his wife getting along?"

"Ooo." The question seemed to surprise Watson. "Oh yes. As far as I know they were—I'm certain they were, yes. They seemed—they've always seemed rather the perfect couple, in fact. Devoted to each other—as far as I know. At least, that's how it seemed to me."

"And he didn't allude to any dispute or disagreement they might be having?"

"Oh, no. Uh—I don't think anybody—well, Christine Harvey might have asked, you know, about her, she being a woman and everything. Men don't—well, you know what I mean. I mean I'm just imagining she probably did. I can't really remember."

****

Neither Lawrence Barrow nor Carver Rockwell, the next two men on the list, were any more helpful. Stark asked them both about Harper's "minor glitch" remark. Barrow didn't remember it at all, and Rockwell said it had seemed to him nothing more than an off-hand remark. Barrow said he had never seen Harper so content and confident and satisfied and echoed Watson's "perfect couple" description, but Rockwell said he thought they might be "getting a little farther apart from each other."

"They used to be in each other's shadows, you see what I mean, but now they seem to be each finding his and her own space. I wouldn't call it a problem. Just the opposite, really. It's like they're becoming more synergistic, sort of concomitantly independent and interdependent, rather than totally relying on each other for support and endorsement, do you see what I mean?"

Stark shook his head.

****

Lunch with Charlie Hayden was what lunch with Charlie Hayden had been the first two times Stark had had occasion to consult him, which made Stark glad he didn't have to see anyone else the rest of the day—not after the pâté and the cream-of-asparagus soup and the grilled tuna and the chocolate gâteau and the martinis and the two bottles of Bordeaux and the three Napoleon brandies. Between the chews and the sips and various sonorous indications of prandial satisfaction, Hayden managed to impart some useful information.

"Pass me the rolls, will you, old boy." Hayden held out an enormous hand to take possession of the bread basket. It was the only size of hand that would have been suitable for such a body.

Hayden was massive, as befitted a former professional wrestler. He had wrestled for a time in England under the name Man-Mountain Martino, the Sicilian Smasher, even though he had been born in Brixton, South London, and didn't speak a word of Italian. But he had dark eyes and thick, black curls, which he said, combined with his size (both his parents being short and dumpy), made him suspect he'd been conceived by a passing sailor.

While he affected the voice of a military officer, he'd never got past lance corporal in the British National Service. He'd gone into wrestling after a stint in London's Metropolitan Police, when a promoter had spotted him boxing in an intra-force match. He'd made a lot more money as a wrestler than he could ever have made as a cop, but his career had been cut short when he'd slipped on a bar of soap in the bathtub and broken his neck. After that, he'd taken a job in the investigations unit of the London Stock Exchange, which led eventually to the Ontario Securities Commission position.

"This Harper killing? You don't think it was a burglar then, as the press reports said? Pour me another drop of that lovely wine, will you, old chap?"

"I don't know for sure, one way or the other."

"Mmm. Well, you wanted to know about Harper and Co., yes?"

"I did, yes, and still do."

"Right. The outfit is BH Exploration Consultants. They're not on the board; they're just a small outfit, a partnership, but let me tell you, they are powerful. The B is a fellow called Shane Bishop. He's the hustler of the duo—they met at university.

"They're both geologists, but Bishop is the businessman. Harper just wants—wanted—to wander around the world looking at rocks. Actually, they are fascinating things, rocks. This tuna is magnificent, don't you think? They do fish wonderfully here." They were dining at Hayden's club, The Albion, which is where they had eaten the last time. "I hope it's all right for you here. No women worth looking at, I'm afraid. I find them forbidding in those dark suits, like nuns, and, being raised a Catholic, I'm terrified of nuns."

"It's very nice, very pleasant."

"Well, I brought you here because I know you like to smoke those smelly cigarettes, and after lunch we can retire—as they say—with our brandies to the smoking room and you can puff away to your heart's content."

"Very civilized."

"Exactly. Course I don't smoke myself, just the occasional cigar, never took it up as a habit, always in athletics, you know, but I would never begrudge a man his pleasure. Both my parents smoked—died from it—oh, sorry."

"That's all right." Stark smiled.

"Do you know there's a movement afoot to close our smoking room? Only lost by ten votes at the last annual meeting. I suspect it's the women are behind it. But you can't keep them out these days. Now, what was I saying?"

"Bishop is the businessman; Harper liked rocks."

"Exactly. Harper had the brains, of course. I think if Bishop doesn't find another partner just as sharp—well, I suppose he'll do all right, but Harper was a geological genius—he was like Midas."

"Yes. He had the cover of the magazine in which they called him Midas framed on his wall."

"Did he indeed?"

"Mmm."

"They were very successful, made big discoveries all over the world, and had a tremendous reputation. Reputation is everything in this business."

"Geology?"

"Mmm, no, not precisely. Exploration. You see, there are two things involved in the mining business. One, of course, is finding the minerals, digging them up and selling them. The other is making money by pushing up the price of your stock."

"And that's where their reputation comes in?"

"Exactly. If you can get BH to say you've got a hot property, whoops, up goes the price of your shares. Now, you asked me about something called X-King."

"Right."

"Sorry, couldn't find anything with a handle like that. However, don't despair, because I think it's a code word, or at least it could be—it has the right ring—for a piece of property BH had been looking at in New Guinea, called Royal Cross."

"Oh yes?"

"Yes. And interestingly enough, we've already started looking into Royal Cross."

"Why's that?"

"Well, it's like this. An outfit called Delsim Mining owns the rights to the property, and lately their stock, for no apparent reason, has taken a couple of serious jumps. In fact, it's been going up pretty steadily. Now, Delsim has not issued any sort of report on the property, they've made no claims at all. So we asked them whether they knew about anything that would cause the stock to jump, but they said they were just as puzzled as we were. Said they were still involved in test drills. But it wouldn't be the first time that a company has started a rumour about the value of a find. Of course, if they have information that there's nothing substantial on the site, they have an obligation to make that information public. Because by not saying anything, they're implying—"

"I understand what you're saying. But if BH is involved, wouldn't they want the information released? If there is nothing in the ground there, I mean their reputation would be at stake, isn't that right?"

"Yes, but it puts them between a rock and a hard place, because they are working for Delsim. They can't really publish the information themselves. If they knew that there was nothing there, and the potential was being implicitly misrepresented, I suppose they could take the bull by the horns and just publish the information. Delsim would hardly be able to sue them successfully for breach of contract. On the other hand, because there's always a certain amount of uncertainty in the mining business, they'd run into real problems if, for instance, Delsim's own people had actually found something, and BH's publishing their findings tumbled the stock. You see what I mean?"

"They'd have to be absolutely sure there couldn't be anything there?"

Hayden nodded. "Yes, and for all we know there could be something. Delsim might have some reason for not releasing the information, although the usual pattern is that you put such information out as quickly as you can and send the stock soaring."

"What is this Delsim outfit? I've never heard of it. Not that that means much. Are they a big company?"

"They're what's called a junior. That covers a pretty wide range, but this outfit is small, even for a junior. In fact, it's an odd thing that they used BH. I don't know how they could afford them. But BH has helped. Delsim's stock was pennies a few months ago, and now it's at eleven dollars."

"So, there's a lot of money at stake."

"For somebody. If they're not too greedy and they time it right. The biggest block of shares was picked up by some developer in Woodbridge." Hayden took out a notebook and flipped it open. "Cataldi Enterprises. I've never heard of it."

"Who are the principals in Delsim? Have you got their names?"

"There's only one really. Bill Bream. He's the president. I can get you a list of the officers if you need it. They're all his family. He's a nice fellow, actually. A dreamer. Struck gold up north somewhere years ago. Has a small mine there, still running, brings in enough to pay the bills. As I recall, they hit a healthy seam a couple of years ago, and he used some of that money to buy the rights to the site in Papua New Guinea."

"Where's their office?"

"I've no idea. I can get you that, too, but I'm sure they're in the phone book, if you're in a hurry. Why do you want to know, anyway? It's none of my business—actually, it is, of course, if they're into any funny business. Do you think they're involved in this somehow?"

"Probably not. But Harper told some friends of his that there was a 'minor glitch,' to quote him, in the business. Maybe Delsim was the minor glitch. Anyway, the way I work is a little weird, Charlie." Stark chuckled. "I'm notorious for it. I collect all kinds of useless information, and sometimes it turns out to be the key to the case. More often than not it's a total waste of time. But that's the way I do it."

"Mmm. I'm going to have some of that chocolate cake on that trolley there. Will you join me? And then we'll go and relax in the smoking room, shall we?"

"Why not?"

Chapter Eight

Stark spent as little time at headquarters as he had to. He went there, to 40 College Street, when he had to interview suspects, and he had to show up every day during the rare times when he wasn't working on a case. The rest of the time he would make a token appearance on the third floor a couple of times a week.

Most of the time, Stark's only contact was by phone, often through the squad's secretary, Marilyn—or by modem. For some time now, Stark had had no partner. For years, his partner had been Bud Craig, a warm bear of a man, as garrulous as Stark was withdrawn. Bud was one of the few who would tolerate Stark's moroseness. He knew that Stark, in the setting and with the company of his own choice, was perfectly companionable. Stark had felt very close to Craig, and when the big man had had a heart attack in their car, he had tried desperately, but futilely, to revive him.

Since then, Stark had had no partner. His inspector had agreed to it—at first on a trial basis—partly because Stark was such a successful investigator and partly because by Stark's working on his own, the unit was able to stretch its thinning resources. Mostly, though, it was because nobody liked to work with Stark anyway, and his fellow detectives half-hoped that on one of his lone-wolf escapades he'd get his come-uppance.

The morning after his lunch with Hayden—which

was followed by several beers at Carbo's, leading to a slightly swaying walk home at ten o'clock and a complete collapse on the couch and, thankfully, a dreamless sleep—he came into the office at seven, checked his mail slot and found an unstamped envelope addressed to him. Marilyn wasn't in yet, so he couldn't ask how it had been delivered. He opened it, read the single sheet of paper it contained, picked up the phone and punched the local extension number for Bob Payne, the headquarters systems guy. Payne, who had no life apart from what he saw on a computer screen, would have been there since about six a.m.

"Talk to me," Payne answered.

"Bobby, Stark."

"Harry. You're in early. What happened? She sober up and throw you out of bed?"

"Something like that. Listen, Bob, I need your expert knowledge. If you're free for an hour or so?"

"Sure."

"I want you to meet me as soon as you can at 45 Carson Avenue. It's in the Beaches."

"Where the guy was killed?"

"That's the place."

"What should I bring? What do you want to do?"

"I want you to try to retrieve some files for me on a PC."

"How old?"

"The PC?"

"No, the files."

"Oh, I think pretty recent."

"Shouldn't be a problem. I'll see you there, eh?"

****

Stark used his roof light to pass the traffic on the

Lake Shore, and was at the house in minutes. He let himself in the front door, and looked again at the note from the envelope in his mail slot. It was made up of words cut from a newspaper and some other publication on coarse stock, but flimsier than regular newsprint, and read "door in wall down stairs Carson." The last two words were from the other publication—a phone book, Stark thought.

If there was a door, it couldn't be in the wall to his right. That was the exterior wall. Straight ahead were two doors, one that led to the downstairs apartment and one that opened to a flight of stairs leading to the Harper/Johnson apartment. Surely, the note couldn't be referring to either of those. The wall on the left was stucco strapped with vertical oak boards, giving a sort of Tudor look. And there it was. It wasn't hard to see it, if you were looking for a door. You wouldn't notice the edges, because they were framed by the oak boards, but about seven feet up on the stucco, there was a horizontal line. You might have thought it was a crack in the stucco. Now, how did it open? That proved easy. One push and a spring catch released and the door popped open about six inches.

"God damn it," he said, and opened it wider. There was a flight of stairs, the walls of which were thick with dust; there were cobwebs in the corners, but the stairs themselves were clean, as if they'd been wiped recently with a cloth. Stark took out a pocket flashlight and shone it up the stairs. They climbed to a landing and then made a ninety-degree right turn.

He went up. At the top, overhead, there was a trap door. He pushed it, but it wouldn't budge. He went back down and climbed the main stairs to the apartment, went to the pantry, opened the door and pulled the chain to turn on the light on the wall. The floor of the pantry was covered with a sheet of linoleum. It was curled at the edges, not fastened down. There were some cartons stacked at the back of the pantry, a plastic pail with a mop stood in it, a broom and a dustpan and brush. There was enough room on the shelves to hold the items from the floor. He put them on the shelves, lifted the lino, slid back a bolt and opened the trap door.

"Well, I'll be—"

"Hello. Harry, you there?"

"That you, Bobby? C'mon in." Stark closed the trap door, put the lino back and returned the stuff he'd put on the shelves to the floor. "I'll be right with you."

Payne was standing on the stairs, knowing that he shouldn't pass the yellow tape into the crime scene without permission.

"C'mon in," Stark said again. "Close the door behind you. The beast is in here." He led the computer expert into the office and pointed at the machine where Harper's body had been found. "That one."

"Boy, this guy's got all the bells and whistles in here eh? Okay, what are we looking for?"

"Well, unless I'm wrong, we should be able to find a file, or a directory, labelled 'X-King.'"

"X-King, as in the letter 'X' and 'king,' all one word?"

"No, I suspect it will be a capital X followed by a hyphen and the word 'King' with a capital 'K.'"

"All right, let's give it a try." Payne pushed a floppy disc into the slot, activated the machine, and entered a series of commands with practised and impressive speed. In a matter of seconds, he had fired up the utilities disc and located the sought name. "It's a directory; there are five files, eh. Uh, here's one."

The file appeared on the screen. Payne was a professional; he immediately pivoted the chair around to avoid reading the words on the screen.

"Can you print that out for me? In fact, print the whole directory. Oh, and can you determine the dates that each file was written?"

"I can tell you the dates that each was last worked on."

"That's fine."

"No problem." Payne punched in some more commands, then began to note down the dates. His fingers moved considerably slower manipulating a ballpoint pen than they had on the computer keyboard. Finally, he turned on the printer, and almost as soon as he'd activated the print command, sheets of paper began to emerge. There were about fifty sheets in the tray when the printing stopped. As each one emerged, Stark had Payne sign them.

"Thanks, old boy," Stark said when the task was completed. He gathered up the sheets and stuffed them in a manila envelope.

"That's it?"

"That's it."

"Good. I'm outta here. So, we'll see you around, Harry."

"Yeah, good stuff, Bobby."

"Aah—nuthin'."

****

Stark phoned Marilyn from the back booth at Holtzman's. Sid Holtzman was sitting across from him, but Stark wasn't concerned that Sid might overhear his conversation. Sid had a one-track mind, and right now that track was devoted to the *Daily Racing Form*. In the past, Stark had seen customers standing at the counter trying to get Sid's attention when he was concentrating on some thinking task. He'd seen them cough, tap the counter with a coin, call out, "Excuse me," all to no avail.

"Marilyn, Stark. Yeah, I'm fine. Listen I want—oh, sorry, how are you? Fine? Good. Now, I got an envelope this morning in my mail slot—yeah, I was in—early.— Well, he'll have to catch me the next time. He got my report—Yeah, never mind that. Listen, the envelope. How did it get there? It wasn't mailed. It was hand-delivered. Did anybody see who delivered it?"

Marilyn told him it would have come up with the intra-office mail, which probably meant it was delivered to the front desk. Stark had her transfer his call. The constable on the front desk remembered the envelope, said it had just appeared on the counter, and he'd put it in the intra-office basket. Didn't see who delivered it.

"We get people coming and going all the time, Sarge. Sometimes there's a whole crowd out here, you know."

"I understand. Okay, that's fine, thanks." He put the cell phone away. "Sid, can I—" He started to ask Sid for a coffee refill, but Sid's head was still occupied, so Stark decided it would be faster and less of a hassle if he got up and poured the coffee himself.

"Can I get you one, Sid?" he said, expecting and receiving no response. He poured two cups, and a cab driver seated at the counter said *he'd* like a refill. Stark shrugged. "Why not?" he said. The cabbie looked up casually, then did a double-take when he saw the man pouring the coffee was wearing a suit.

Stark gave him a clown smile, and took *his* coffee and Sid's back to the booth. Sid didn't appear to notice, but after making a couple of more pencil marks, he took a sip of the coffee without taking his eyes off the paper. He looked at Stark, screwed up his face and made a sound of disgust. "There's no sugar," he said. Stark shook his head and looked at the ceiling.

****

The material that had been printed from Harper's computer was nearly all unreadable to Stark—all highly technical. The only sheet he could understand was a short letter addressed to Shane Bishop.

"I'm not going to let this X-King thing ride. Our reputation is going to go down the tubes. I don't care how much money is involved. We have an obligation to reveal what we know. I don't want to have to do it on my own, but I will if you don't agree. You've got three days."

Stark checked the list of dates Payne had made. The letter was last worked on the Thursday before the Sunday Harper was killed.

"Well, what do you know."

Chapter Nine

Lunch with Christine Harvey was nothing like lunch with Charlie Hayden. In fact, the contrast was so remarkable, Stark chuckled to himself about it. They met in a lunch bar off Adelaide Street. The only beverages offered were bottled water, juices and herbal tea. There was a huge sign that said "Smoke-Free Zone." Stark's tuna sandwich contained more alfalfa sprouts than tuna and was served on unevenly cut, thick slices of something called granary bread.

"I think they forgot to grind the grain," he said.

Harvey didn't seem to get it. She smiled and nodded, taking another mouthful of undressed salad.

"Yes, it's good, isn't it?" She had a strikingly beautiful face. Her hair was cropped short. She wore no make-up, but she had natural colour in her complexion, high cheekbones and unclipped, thin, arching eyebrows, beneath which dark eyes darted with nervous energy. Her voice was rich and husky, and Stark had trouble concentrating on her words for the sound of them.

But what he did hear suggested she hadn't been at the same gathering as the rest of Harper's friends, and that the Harper she'd known wasn't the same one they had known.

"Something was really bothering him. He was disturbed. Something about his partner, Bishop, I think."

"Did he say anything specific?"

"No. It was just his manner. Distracted. They weren't a happy couple, you know, despite what everybody thinks."

"Who? Harper and Bishop?"

She raised her eyebrows, and then said, "No, I mean Chris and Dianne."

"They weren't?"

Harvey sighed and took a sip of spring water from the neck of a plastic bottle. Stark raised his cup of camomile tea, looked at it and put it down without drinking. He had already abandoned his sandwich. "She tried. Dianne tried. But—"

"But what? He had another woman?"

"Hmm. Not exactly."

"Not exactly? Well, exactly what?"

"Exactly, he had another man. That is, he had a *man*."

"Are you saying Harper was gay?"

"That's right. He and Bishop, his partner."

"You're kidding?"

"I'm sorry. Why would I be kidding? You think that's impossible?"

"Well, no, it's—no, not at all. It's just that—well, you're the first one to suggest this. How do you know?"

"They knew each other at university, you know, long before Chris met Dianne. I went to school with them, too. I knew them both. They were roommates. Later on, after they'd set up their partnership, Bishop wanted Chris to move in with him, in the house on Carson."

"In their house? The one they lived in?"

"Yes. Bishop lived there first, by himself. And then when Chris announced he was getting married, Bishop did 'the decent thing.' He moved out, let them take it over. He was just being a martyr. He's sulky. He broods."

"You knew them at university. Were they—a couple then?"

"They kept it quiet, but—yes."

"I'm a bit naive about this stuff, but if Chris Harper was a homosexual, why did he—get married?"

She shrugged. "Chris was bisexual. He liked Dianne—he fell in love with her, I guess."

"Did you know Dianne Johnson well? Did she tell you—"

"No. She didn't tell me."

"I was going to say—well, you said she tried—tried what?"

"I knew about it—mostly through Chris. Things he said. She was always—helping him. You know. She was trying—I guess to make it work, to make the marriage work. That's all. Look, I have to get back to work. If there's nothing else—"

"Wait a second, wait a second. Take it easy." Stark tried another bite of the sandwich and then completely abandoned it. "Let me ask you this, *Ms* Harvey, whom do *you* think killed Harper?"

She stared at him for an instant. "A burglar, wasn't it?" she said, eyebrows raised, in a tone that suggested she didn't think much of the idea.

"You don't think so?"

"I know it wasn't."

"Is this, I'm sorry, a—theory, or—"

"Look, Mr Stark, if you think that I'm—"

"No, no—No, tell me. Who do you think killed him?"

"I can't get sued, can I?"

"As long as you tell only me, you can't, no."

"Okay, then I think Shane Bishop killed him."

Stark took a deep breath, let it go with a whoosh. "Whoo. All right then. Why? What the hell for?"

Harvey looked down at the table, then raised her eyes and looked hard at Stark. "You know something? I really don't have a clue." She shook her head. "Not really. It's just—a gut feeling. It's because—well, who else? I mean, you know, it's almost always somebody you know, right?—Somebody you *love*—" She stressed the word "love," twisting her lips "—It's somebody you love who kills you, isn't it?"

Stark shook his head "And that's it? That's your whole—that's what you're basing your accusation on?"

"Yes, that's it. And it's not an accusation. You asked me, and I told you. Now, is there anything else? I really have to go."

"No, no. Wait a minute. Accusing somebody of murder is a pretty serious thing. You've got to have real reasons for it. Come on. So, tell me. Why do you think Bishop killed him?"

She squirmed in her seat, bit her lip. Her eyes narrowed. And then the words came out like a burst of gunfire. "Because Bishop is a bastard. Because Chris was always having problems with him. Shane was always trying to pull some fast one. I think Chris was going to dump him. At the party, he said something about a problem he was having with his business—"

"A minor glitch?"

"Yes. I think he did use those words. But you had to watch his face when he said it. There was nothing *minor* in his expression. I think he was going to dump Bishop.

85

Not only as a partner, but as a lover, too. And Bishop couldn't survive without him. Bishop's finished now—without Chris. Chris had all the brains. Bishop's an idiot. I'm sure he cheated his way through school. I know he bought papers. He tried to buy an old one of mine once. I told him to fuck off. I don't think you've met Bishop yet, or have you?"

"No."

"Well, you wait till you see him. He's a complete phony."

"Tell me—how do you know that he and Harper were still—lovers?"

She stared out the window. Finally, she said, "Look. I do know Dianne a little. She called me once. I guess she had no one else to speak to—no other woman. I don't think she could talk to her sister. Her sister doesn't have much—understanding. Anyway, she told me that she suspected Chris and Bishop were having an affair. That's how I know."

"Funny, she didn't tell *me* that."

"Well, she wouldn't, would she?"

"Don't you think she'd have the same suspicions as you?"

"I—I don't know. Ask her. Now, I do have to go."

"Yeah, Okay. Listen, I may have to talk to you again."

She sighed. "All right. Oh—thanks for the lunch. I see yours didn't agree with you." She lifted her eyebrows without smiling.

Stark watched her walk out of the restaurant. She had on a calf-length denim skirt and a short, down-filled jacket, which she'd unzipped but not taken off while they were eating. Beneath the jacket, she wore a bulky wool sweater with a high roll collar. The fact that despite the looseness of her clothing, you could still make out the shape of her body suggested to Stark that it must be an ample body, and he couldn't help wondering.

****

Stark got a call from the coroner's office. Jennifer Johnson had called them and asked whether the body could be released for burial. Stark gave his assent.

Bishop was in the BH office when Stark phoned, and agreed to see him right away.

The office was on the second floor of a converted house near King and Parliament. It was austere and unwelcoming—bare, eggshell walls; unstained, varnished hardwood floor; pristine—not an errant sheet of paper, in fact, barely any paper; not a dirty coffee cup, or a coffee cup at all, for that matter; nothing out of place; hardly anything to have in place. Ordered.

Bishop was a big man, tall, more than six feet; pear-shaped, with a long torso and a head that seemed too far away from his belt and too small for his body, as if the maker mixed up the order. His hair was dark and pulled back severely into a pony tail. It seemed to have drawn his face with it, an effect rendered by his eyebrows' being thin and arched and high on his forehead. The hair colour contrasted with, accentuated, the paleness of his skin, unmarked and unwrinkled, enhancing the effect of its being stretched by the pony tail. His mouth was tiny and straight and thin, and his upper lip didn't move when he spoke, his jaw dropping and lifting, like a marionette's.

"Mr Stark, is it?" Shane Bishop said with a sigh, as if speaking was painful.

"That's right."

"Listen, I'm sorry about the other day." He sighed again. "I was just—I was devastated. Chris and I were very close. We've known each other since school. We started this business together. We've always been— together. Take a seat, will you, Mr—uh, Stark. Right there," he said absurdly, since apart from two office chairs at their respective desks, one of which Bishop was rolling out to sit on, there was only one other chair in the place, an uncomfortable-looking, low-slung canvas affair, shaped like a distorted figure eight. Stark assessed it, and thought he'd feel and look like a fool with his rear end almost on the floor and having to look through his knees at Bishop.

"I think I'll sit over here," he said, and pulled out the other office chair.

"That was Chris's," Bishop said, with a ridiculous little squeal that made Stark's stomach tighten.

"Mr Bishop, I won't take up much of your time. There are only a few things. I'll keep it very short. First, tell me, how was business?"

"Business?" He had a quizzical look. "Business was—terrific, fabulous, couldn't have been better. But— I don't quite understand—what does that have to do with Chris's murder? I thought you were here—"

"Well, never mind, Mr Bishop. That'll be fine. Business was good, you say. Tell me, Mr Bishop, did you and Mr Harper have any—disagreements over business matters?"

"No, not at all—never. Well, you know, there's always some minor—"

"Glitches?"

"Well, I wouldn't have used that word, but perhaps you could call it that."

"Like what, for instance?"

"Well, like—Mr Stark, I don't see what any of this has to do with Chris's murder. That is what you're investigating, isn't it?"

"Why? Is there something else I should be investigating?"

"No, of course not. But—really, our business affairs certainly had nothing to do with a burglar smashing my partner on the head. I mean, if he'd been killed here at the office, then perhaps I could see—even then, it would be absurd—but he was killed at home, by somebody who broke in, some stranger."

"Is there some reason you don't want to tell me about the business disagreement, Mr Bishop?"

"No, no." He shook his head violently and glared at Stark, then, emphasizing each word, he said: "What business disagreement? There are no business problems."

"You said there were."

"That was a—you know, a passing remark. I shouldn't have said it. Please forget it." He took a deep breath and let it out. "Look, what else do you want to know? I must say, I think your line of questioning is quite ridiculous."

Stark stared at him for a time, then looked at a blank page in his notebook as if he was consulting something, and asked, "When was the last time you saw him?"

"Chris? I saw him—let me think—a week ago last Friday."

"That long? Was he out of town?"

"Not at all. He mostly works from home, you see. The thing is we do—God, we *did* most of our work on computers. I use this one. I basically run the office, I run the business end of the business. Chris did most of the geology, and because it gets awkward to bring things back and forth, he did nearly all of his work at home. He was in the office—you know, for regular business matters—last Friday, a week ago Friday, as I said."

"And that was the last—did you speak to him on the phone?"

"Oh sure, every day, several times a day. Always."

Stark pretended to consult his notes again. He closed the notebook and looked hard at Bishop. "Do you think anyone besides a burglar would have a reason to kill Harper?"

"What? No, that's absurd. Whatever for? He had no—enemies. Isn't that what you people ask about? Well, he had none. He was a mild-mannered, gentle person, a gentleman. He was devoted to his wife and he was devoted to his work. He didn't gamble; he didn't drink—I mean to excess. He never took drugs in his life, even at university. He was athletic; he liked to hike and ski and that sort of thing."

Bishop put his head back and looked at one corner of the ceiling and another, as if he were checking for cobwebs. Then he lowered his eyes and his head stopped moving and he looked at Stark, held the palm of a hand out and almost pleaded: "I—I don't know what else to say."

Stark said: "What about you, Mr Bishop, do you like to hike and ski?"

Bishop screwed up his face in a look that clearly meant, "What the hell does that have to do with anything?" but in the end, in a tone that carried the same meaning, said, "Yes, a little. Sometimes I hike on Sunday afternoon." He adjusted two books on the desk in front of him, so they were evenly stacked.

"Chris was—he was a gentleman, Mr Stark. No one who knew him would want, would have any possible reason to kill him. You're looking for a burglar, Mr Stark, or a crazy person. Perhaps it was somebody deranged. I don't know. But I do know you're wasting your time if you look anywhere else. The idea is just, well, it's ridiculous. As I said, I'm afraid these questions you're asking—"

Stark raised a hand. "All right, Mr Bishop." He flipped his notebook open and closed. "I won't ask any more absurd questions. I think you've answered any that I might have had. And I want to thank you. Sorry to have upset you."

Bishop shook his head dismissively. "No, no, that's—you're just doing your job. I just hope you find whoever did this—before he kills somebody else."

Chapter Ten

Stark was ensconced in his usual stool at the piano bar. Morty was just finishing up a rich rendition of "Moonglow" and weaving in "Theme From Picnic," with lots of flourishes and long runs, as the finale to a medley of movie themes for the early-evening diners, most of whom were ignoring him.

Ulysses, unnecessarily, insisted on what he called "Light stuff with no singing." between six and nine. Morty, being a professional, would have played those kinds of selections anyway. He announced his movie medley as being "from the time when they actually wrote real music for films." Stark had encouraged him with a "Yeah, right." No one else had heard Morty's announcement.

"Morty said, "What do you want to hear now, Harold?"

"How about a little Chopin?"

"You must be kidding, for this crowd? Suggest something realistic."

"'Detour Ahead.'"

"No, screw that. I'll save the good stuff till later, till these clods stop munching and drink themselves into a stupor, so only the good people are left listening. How about 'Moon River?'" He laughed. "I think I'll do 'Moon River.' No, I'll do a Beatles thing. They think that's classical music. Hey, watch this."

He pulled the mike close to his mouth and looked toward the nearest table of diners at which two young couples were chewing hard on Ulysses' souvlaki and looking as if they'd spent too much time in each other's company. "For the lovely lady in the green dress—you, with the divine curls—yes you, my dear. A dedication from someone in the room who wanted you to hear this and listen to the lyrics."

The woman looked questioningly at her companions, then grinned inanely, shrugging her shoulders and looking around to see whether anyone was looking at her. Morty began to play "I Want to Hold Your Hand," at such a slow, ballad-like pace, it took half the tune before they recognized it. Then the girl began to question her husband, who shook his head and twisted his mouth in puzzlement. The others shook their heads in turn.

Throughout, Stark was watching in amusement. Finally, when Morty finished, the woman took off her napkin and came over to Morty.

"Hello, my dear. I hope you liked that."

She gave a weak smile. "Yes, it was—nice, but who—you said somebody—dedicated that to me. Who?"

"I'm sorry, my dear. I didn't see who it was. He came up behind me and whispered in my ear. I didn't turn around. I'm sorry. Obviously, he's somewhere in the room." Morty smiled affectedly. The girl scanned the crowd, then smiled at Morty again, said, "Thank you," and went back to her table, at which everyone, especially her husband, leaned conspiratorially toward the centre, and then all began to look around the room, trying to spot a likely culprit.

"You are a sonofabitch," Stark said to Morty, whose

head was ducked, his hand over his mouth, concealing the giggles.

"I know, but it's so much fun. With any luck, the husband will think he's found the guy. Some poor sap will look at his wife and we'll have a donnybrook."

"God, you must be bored."

Morty sighed, and then grinned widely as he started a Beatles medley.

Stark shook his head. He felt something press against his back, froze when he realized it was Sharon's breasts pressing into his back as she leaned over him to deposit Morty's white wine.

"Can I get you a refill?" she asked Stark.

"Christ, you can get me anything you want, Sharon," he said.

"What do you mean?" she said, with no suggestion of hidden meaning.

"Yeah, I'll have the same again," he said, shaking his head. "She doesn't know," Stark said after she'd moved out of earshot.

"Yes, I saw your eyes light up." Morty gave him a condescending look. "You're so bloody juvenile. A woman accidentally touches you with her bust, and you go into heat."

"Never mind that. I like it. I wouldn't expect *you* to understand. Anyway, I don't think she does know. She's a big farm girl from Dagmar or someplace up there. I don't think she has any idea. But, I'm not going to tell her."

"Where the hell's Dagmar?"

"Never mind, Morty. It's in what they call the *country*. You must have seen pictures of it. You know, it's where they have fields and cows and that sort of thing."

Sharon brought the drinks. This time she leaned more carefully, not touching Stark at all. He smiled.

"Maybe she does know. Maybe I blew it."

"God, you're pathetic. Oh look at the couple. They're arguing. Oh geez, they're getting up to leave. It's a riot."

"And you're calling me juvenile?"

"Oh shut up."

****

"His name's Horace MacIver—Chilly, they call him, because he's always complaining about the cold—summer and winter." A sergeant from 52 Division had called Stark's cell phone and left a message. "The other guy's Carl Ellison, the druggie, the one who tried to sell the cards to the undercover, but I don't think you'd be interested in him. Chilly's the one who found the wallet. We've got him here if you want to interview him. As soon as I saw the name, I recognized it as the Beaches guy. We picked Chilly up five minutes after the guy gave us the description. You'll see why when you see him."

And Stark did see why—a long ugly scar down the left side of his face, his left eye permanently half-closed by it.

"Why do they keep this place so fuckin' cold, Cap'n? Jesus."

"Fuel's expensive, Chilly. I guess they got to keep costs down. Budget's tight, you know."

"Yeah, I—I guess that's it, eh?"

"Probably. Can I get you a coffee, Chilly? Sandwich, maybe?"

"Wouldn't mind, actually, Cap'n. Long as I don't have to pray or nuthin'." Chilly grinned at his own quip.

His face exploded in wrinkles, like a crumpled brown paper bag. The crease of the scar deepened, and his half-closed eye shut altogether. In the centre of his face was a black hole of a mouth, with snags and stumps and a wide gap that several of his front teeth no longer occupied.

The effect was a striking aggregate of humour and horror that Stark felt would have been perfect for a thriller movie. In fact, a film company *had* discovered Chilly on the street and used him for exactly that purpose, and Chilly had gone around telling his friends he had a part in a movie. The trouble was he couldn't remember the name of it, so nobody believed him, and he never did get to see himself on the screen—not that he or his acquaintances had been in a movie theatre for years. "If you've got baloney, I'll have baloney, or cheese, you know, whatever you've got'll be fine, Cap'n. And tea maybe—you got tea? If you don't—"

"I'll get you tea, Chilly. Tea it is." Stark stuck his head out the door of the interview room and gave the order to the nearest constable, who looked put out at having to be a waiter for some detective who didn't work in his station, but he grudgingly did what he was asked.

Stark cautioned Chilly, asked him whether he wanted to speak to a lawyer.

"I don't need no god-damned lawyer, Cap'n. I ain't done nothin' wrong. 'Sides, I don't trust the bastards."

Stark switched on the tape recorder, spoke the time and location, identified himself and asked Chilly to identify himself.

"I thought you knew who I was?"

"For the tape, Chilly."

"Oh." Chilly beamed with self-importance and said

loudly: "Horace Jerome MacIver." He gave an approval-seeking nod to Stark.

"That's fine, Chilly. So tell me, did you like it in the Beaches?"

"The what?"

"The Beaches, Chilly, you know, in the East End. Queen Street. You know the Beaches, Chilly. You've been there recently, haven't you?"

"I don't know no fuckin' beach, man. Toronto doesn't have no fuckin' beach. Pardon my French. I mean, not that you'd swim at or nuthin', eh. It's too f—too cold, man. The water's too—damn cold."

"C'mon, Chilly, you've been to the Beaches. Let's see how maybe you got there. Maybe you were feeling adventurous one day, or maybe you'd had a run-in with one of your chums, right? So you decided to get out of your stomping grounds for a while, and maybe you wandered south and found yourself along at Cherry Beach. It's not far. You just keep walking past the harbour, you know where the big ships are—"

"Wait a minute, wait a minute. You're talking to me like I'm a fuckin'—like I'm an idiot. 'Where the big ships are.' I know what a harbour is, man. I was in the Navy, fightin' fer this country eleven years, eh. I was all over the world. In Cyprus. I been to Cyprus and—Bermuda. You ever been to Bermuda? It's nice there—warm, nice and warm, eh. A hell of a lot warmer than it is in this fuckin' place, I'll tell ya."

"Okay, Chilly, you're not an idiot. You're a war hero—"

"I didn't say I was no hero."

"You were in the Navy. So, if you were in the Navy, you've got a good sense of direction, right, Chilly?"

He shrugged. "I guess so."

"So you know when you've been to the East End."

"I ain't never been there, Cap'n. I can tell you that right now."

"Chilly, that's where you got the wallet."

"No, it ain't."

"Yes it is. Here's what I think happened, Chilly. I think that somehow you ended up in the East End. Maybe you climbed under the tarp in a truck to get warm, and the guy drove off with you in there, and you got out somewhere along Queen Street, and it was dark and it was cold and you didn't know the area, you didn't know any of the sheltering spots, so you wandered into a back yard—"

"Hey, this is a good story, but—"

"And when you were in the backyard, you spotted a light on the second floor of a house, and you saw these metal stairs, and at the top of the stairs, there was a little porch affair, and you figured it'd be easy to break in there, but you didn't have to, because it was unlocked, and when you got in there, it was like a bonanza, because there was a motherlode of wine—"

"Oh, *yeah?*" Chilly grinned. "Shit, I wish I *had* been there. Say, where is this place?"

"So you had yourself a skinful of wine and you got to feeling pretty bold, and you figured why not see if there's anything inside worth taking, and you crept in, and you saw a door was closed, and you opened it quietly, and then you were in trouble."

"I was?"

"You were, because there was a man sitting in there, Chilly. But he was looking the other way, working on a computer, and you had to do something quick before he turned around and caught you, so you rushed in and smashed him—" Stark brought his hand down hard on the table Chilly was sitting at, and Chilly jumped.

"Jesus!"

"And then, Chilly, there was a bonus. Because you saw his wallet. *This* wallet." Stark held it up. "This wallet was sticking out of the back of this fellow's pocket, so you plucked it out, and then eventually you sold the credit cards—and here you are. What do you think of that story, Chilly? You think that's a story? I don't think that's a story. Maybe I haven't got it exactly right, but you're going to straighten me out on it, aren't you, Chilly? Aren't you?"

"Oh, I'm goin' to straighten you out all right, believe me. I'm going to straighten you out—ah, room service." He grinned as the constable brought in the sandwich, wrapped in plastic on a paper plate, tossed it on the far end of the table, put the styrofoam cup of tea beside it, gave Stark a withering look and left.

Chilly looked at the sandwich and then at Stark. Stark made no move toward the sandwich.

"Say, can I—?" Chilly nodded toward the food.

"Can you what, Chilly? You want that sandwich. Wasn't that nice of me to get you a sandwich, Chilly? Now, how about you be nice to me and stop pissing around. Tell me what happened, Chilly, and then you can have your sandwich and your tea."

Chilly smiled wryly, his head nodding. "Wait a minute, what—do you think I'm goin' to confess for a fuckin' baloney sandwich? Give me a break, eh. Jesus Christ."

Stark shook his head, walked slowly to the other end of the table, looked at Chilly and slid the sandwich toward him. He carried the tea back and put it beside Chilly.

Chilly had half the sandwich in his mouth in two bites, mumbled something inaudible, flipped the lid off the tea and slurped a gulp of it noisily. "Hey, there's no milk—oh, never mind, never mind."

"C'mon, Chilly, talk. I'm losing patience here. There's a lot of shit going on, which I don't have time for. Now tell me what happened."

Chilly was on the second half of the sandwich. He was taking his time with this one, nibbling at it. He grinned, revealing a partly chewed lump of sandwich on his tongue.

Stark leaned on the table and glared at him. "Put the sandwich down, Chilly." Chilly looked at him uncertainly, the sandwich held at his mouth, his mouth open. He took another bite. "God damn it, put the sandwich down, Chilly." Chilly paused. Stark slammed his hand on the table and shouted, "Put the fucking thing down."

Chilly tossed the remainder of the sandwich onto the paper plate as if it had caught fire.

"Now talk, Chilly. Talk."

"Sure, I'll talk, but you ain't goin' to like it."

"Never mind whether I like it—"

"Okay, okay. I found it."

"You found it?"

"Yeah, I found the wallet. I didn't do nothin' illegal. It was lyin' there—in an alley—I came along—I picked it up—there was no one around—it's mine. You see, I told you I was in the Navy. I know about these things. It's called the law of salvage. You find something and there's nobody around who says 'It's mine,' then it's yours."

Stark shook his head. "You found it?"

"That's right."

"Where?"

"In an alley up near Wellesley. I don't know the alley. I mean I know the alley, but I don't know—like a name for it, or anything. I can show you."

"You trying to tell me that a wallet that was in the back pocket of a man who got murdered in his apartment in the Beaches magically pops up in an alley downtown?"

"Hey, wait, you ever thought of this, eh? The guy who did the deed, he took the wallet. He got nervous and he threw it away in the alley. And I found it there. What about that, eh?"

"You know what I think about that, Chilly? I think it's bullshit, complete and total bullshit. That's what I think, Chilly. I think you're lying through your—" Chilly smiled. Stark sighed. "Yeah right. Okay, if you found the wallet, Chilly, why didn't you turn it in to a policeman? I know that's a stupid question, but—"

"No-no, it ain't a stupid question, but I already give you the answer, Cap'n. You know—salvage."

"Ah, c'mon, Chilly, you're not that stupid. It was an alley, for Christ's sake, not the middle of the bloody Atlantic Ocean."

"You mean it ain't the same?" Chilly grinned.

"Chilly, you're trying my patience. I'm going to charge you with first-degree murder and then I'm going to have Big Mo come in here and ask you some questions."

"Who?"

"Big Mo."

"Who the hell is that?"

"Big Mo? He's our interrogation expert. Used to be with the Airborne. You remember the Airborne. Remember the Somali kid got killed?"

Chilly looked blank. He shrugged. He probably had no idea what Stark was talking about.

"No, I guess you're not all that up-to-date on current affairs, are you, Chilly?"

Chilly shrugged again.

"Well, Big Mo's a very mean sonofabitch, Chilly. Next to Big Mo, I'm a Salvation Army lady."

"Some of *them* can be pretty—"

"Never mind, Chilly. What I'm saying is, you're going to tell us the truth sooner or later. Why not be smart and make it sooner? Why not save yourself an awful lot of pain? That would be the smart thing to do, Chilly. And I think you're pretty smart."

Chilly raised his eyebrows and inclined his head as if he was thinking about the remark. Then he laughed sardonically and shook his head. "You know, Cap'n, you say you think I'm smart, but you don't treat me like you think I'm smart. Big Mo. That's a god-damned joke, Cap'n. There ain't no Big Mo. You're trying to get me to say something could get me in trouble. All this bullshit about a murder. You think I stole this wallet here, and you want me to say so. Well, I'm tellin' ya, I found it. I ain't goin' to say anything different, and there ain't nothin' you can do to me fer findin' a wallet, so why don't you just let old Chilly go? How about it, Cap'n?"

****

Stark figured that having Chilly locked up for the weekend would have an effect. The officers investigating the sale of the credit cards called for a justice of the peace and had Chilly remanded for a show-cause hearing on Monday morning.

Stark was driving along Queen Street East later, when he saw a woman get off a streetcar and turn down Carson Avenue. "What the hell is she doing?" He asked the dispatcher to find Weems or Cory and have one of them call him on his cell phone. The phone rang within thirty seconds. It was Cory.

"Didn't you tell the Johnson woman that she was to stay away from her apartment until I gave her the go-ahead—I myself, personally?"

"I told her you were in charge of the case and she couldn't go back until you said it was okay. Why?"

"I think I just saw her—well, I think it was her—heading there. All right, thanks. I just wanted to know how things stood—you're sure you made it clear?"

"Absolutely."

"Thanks."

Stark swung the car around and turned on to Carson. She was nowhere in sight. The house was only a few doors down from the corner. He pulled up in front and hurried up the walk, fishing the key out his pocket.

The door into the foyer was open. The police tape was still in place across the stairwell. He ducked under it and climbed the stairs, keeping close to the wall to try to avoid creaking steps. The door at the top of the stairs had been left open a crack, as if the intention was to go in, get something and leave right away. He pushed it open slowly, slipped beneath the tape.

The office door was open. He remembered he'd closed it. He looked inside, and did a double-take. For an instant he thought his imagination was playing tricks. He thought he saw the murdered man still slumped over the keyboard.

There was a man sitting there, but he was alive and his fingers were punching the keys. There was a bald patch on the back of his head, made triangular by the hair's being pulled tautly into a pony tail. Stark started to reach for his gun, but his hand stopped in front of his chest.

He began to perspire, his hands were clammy, his heart pounded, his breathing quickened. He strained mentally to grab the weapon, but Matthew Hardcastle's face flashed on the back of the man's head and he couldn't do it.

Finally, he shouted, "Don't move a fucking muscle." The man's head jerked up and froze. "Put your hands on top of the screen." The man did as he was told. Stark walked into the room, went up behind the man, reached around and felt for a weapon. Finding none, he took out his handcuffs and told the man to put his left hand on top of his head.

The flash of light, the wave of pain, the burst of crimson that turned white and then black were almost simultaneous. Stark saw them in reverse order later, after what seemed like hours, but was less than a minute, when he raised himself on one elbow and looked around the room.

His vision was fuzzy. He pushed himself to a sitting position, felt a throbbing pain from high on his neck just beneath his skull. He shook his head and waited till he could focus.

The room was empty. He felt the back of his head and neck. No blood; the skin wasn't broken. Somebody had hit him expertly, probably without a weapon, but with the edge of his hand, somebody with knowledge of martial arts. He'd been hit hard enough to knock him out, but not hard enough to do any serious damage. In fact, any sensation of his having been slugged all but disappeared within a couple of minutes, except for a lingering pain at the back of his neck and a dull, throbbing headache.

He struggled to his feet, stood unsteadily for a moment, then went straight to the computer, turned it on and tried to fire up Windows. Nothing. The entire system had been cleaned out, wiped, deleted, gone.

"Son of a bitch."

****

When Stark got home, the message light was flashing on his phone. He pressed the right buttons, told the too-perfect recorded voice to "hurry up, for Christ's sake," and then heard Charlie Hayden's rich, mellifluous tone, greeting him with a "How are you, old boy?"

"Not so good, Charlie, it's my sciatica," he said in a weak attempt at humour, made much weaker because it was against what his still addled brain hadn't immediately recognized as the recorded voice of Hayden, saying:

"You expressed interest in a company called Delsim at our lunch the other day, which incidentally was most enjoyable. There are some developments I thought you might be interested in. There have been a number of relatively large purchases of Delsim stock recently. I wasn't aware of this when I spoke to you, but my people had done a little fifth-column work and managed to discover that the people who bought the stock are all very close to that Cataldi Enterprises outfit I told you about up in Woodbridge.

"They're all his cousins—the fellow's name is

Salvatore Cataldi—or his employees—even his mother. The purchases are big enough that if they were made by a single buyer, that person would own enough stock in the company that his name would have to be made public. If we hadn't had an eye on this outfit and hadn't done a little espionage, we'd have never found the link to him.

"It looks like he's not only trying to acquire as much as he can without disclosing, but also he could be trying to pump up the stock. There's some selling among them. It's called churning—each purchase is at a slightly higher price than previous. We've asked Delsim for information again, but I think they're going to continue to play dumb. I don't know whether this ties in with your investigation, but there you are. Let's not be strangers. See you soon, old boy."

Stark put a call through to Ernie Kowalski, his only really close friend on the force since the death of Bud Craig. Kowalski was a detective with the Intelligence Unit. Like himself, Ernie was an outsider. Unconventional. Didn't follow procedure. His superiors didn't like him, projected their dislike to suspicion. Kept trying to prove he was on the take.

Ernie was a gambler, played the horses, went to the casino in Nassau twice a year. And he won—regularly, steadily, almost always. Then he invested his winnings, with the same cunning and luck that he applied to gambling—with the result that he was independently wealthy.

Unlike Stark, Ernie was a team player—at least within his squad. As much as the bosses didn't like him, his fellow officers did: they supported him and protected him from the brass. Ernie was a clown, a buffoon, but it was contrived, an act concealing a brilliant mind. He was a thinker and a reader and an interesting conversationalist. Stark was the only one in the department who knew something else about Ernie Kowalski, something he'd discovered only when he took Ernie to hear Morty Greenwood at Carbo's—Ernie was gay. Stark found it amusing that Kowalski was an arm-punching, one-of-the-boys type, and because Kowalski had confided in him, he felt particularly close.

"Stark, how the hell are you? What's goin' down?"

"Howdy, Ernie. Listen, what do you know about an outfit called Cataldi Enterprises?"

"Salvatore Cataldi?"

"That's the name."

"Quite a dude. Slick Salvatore Cataldi. Very big player, also very smart cat. We got zip on him. Nothing. He's not a made guy, or anything. His mother's a Jew, so he can't be made. Strictly speaking, he's not in the rackets. His business is legit. He builds houses and shit. But the *way* he does business—that's not always quite kosher, you understand.

"He has some unusual methods, and some of his associates are not the most upstanding citizens, you know what I mean? He's not averse to making use of his associates to produce certain results that are favourable to his financial well-being. But we, as I say, have never come up with anything to nail him on. He's a big buddy with a lot of politicians, not all local either. Some in Ottawa. Friends in high places, don't you know? Has some influential friends in the Italian community. Gives a lot to Italian charities. So, why's Homicide interested in Slick Sal? Got his moniker, by the way, because he's got an MBA from Laurier, looks like Robert De Niro and dresses like a hip banker. How'd you run across him?"

"I tell you what, Ernie, it's too complicated to lay on you now. But I'll tell you all about it over a beer. I'll give you a call in the next day or so."

"Hey man, wonderful idea. I'll be waiting."

Stark called Charlie Hayden at home. He asked Hayden whether he could put him on to a good geologist.

Chapter Eleven

Monday morning, Stark went to see Professor Timothy Thomas at the University of Toronto. His office reminded Stark of the old geology gallery at the Royal Ontario Museum. The museum was a frequent family-outing spot when Stark was a kid. He loved the place then, and he thought they had ruined it by making it "user-friendly." He preferred it when it was an echoing labyrinth with row after row of glass display cases filled with items that provided no clue as to their origin and significance beyond little label cards, like "Sword, Ming Dynasty," and so on.

The museum was not a place you went to learn. It was a place you went for atmosphere, a place to stimulate your imagination—another world, with muffled voices and the click of unseen heels on the terrazzo floor from adjoining rooms in the mysterious maze. And the horizontal cases with myriad spectacular butterflies and massive, fuzzy moths—and rocks, thousands of rocks, mute, jagged, brilliant, like the brimming treasure chest of an ancient sultan.

Thomas's office was like that, lined with dusty mahogany racks full of rocks, and hung with renderings of cutaway views of terrain and the entire planet sliced to show its coloured rings, like the hard blackball candies of Stark's childhood.

Thomas himself was like an old rock, weathered and

striated, with a great white beard, yellowed at the corners of his mouth from cigarettes, one of which he was smoking—illegally (by the sacred decrees of the university and the laws of the province) as Stark entered.

"Homicide, eh? Are you here to arrest me for killing my students with second-hand smoke? With some of these little pricks, I'd be doing the world a favour. So, what can I do for you—Detective Harry Stark, I believe I have the honour to address, or so I'm informed by my old friend Charlie Hayden. You know Charlie? Of course, you must know who he is, but do you know him?"

"Fairly well."

"Wonderful chap. Knows how to enjoy life. So few left nowadays."

"I agree."

"You don't mind the—" he held up the smouldering cigarette.

"Not at all, do you mind if I—" Stark showed him his pack of Gauloises.

"Aha, Frenchies. Sure. Stink the place out. They can't get rid of me, anyway. I just growl at the prissy little assholes. What can I do for you, Detective?"

Stark removed the X-King files from an attaché case and threw them on Thomas's desk.

Thomas looked through them quickly. Stark watched his yellowed finger run down each page. Occasionally, he murmured an "mmm," and nodded. When he'd finished, he looked up. "Yeah, so?" he said.

Stark smiled. "Well, what do they say?"

"What do they say? Well, they say that this place, wherever it is—where is it, anyway?"

"Papua New Guinea."

"Oh, New Guinea. Well, in brief, they say there's

nothing there worth bothering about—in terms of minable ore. Nothing economically feasible. You see the way the formation is here?"

"Mmm."

"Well, this is high up, and this is the land that was examined. I imagine this is the area the outfit has the rights to, and if you read this, it tells you that if there *is* any ore worthwhile, it's down here—down in the valley, which apparently, they don't have a piece of. So, this is saying, 'Don't waste your time.'"

"Uh huh. But is it very definite about that? I mean, does it suggest that at first glance, we couldn't find anything, but there's still a possibility—"

"No, no, it's unequivocal. It says there's not a god-damned thing here but rock. With about a million pneumatic chisels, you might have a big frigging gravel pit, but that's about it. This is pretty good work, by the way. Who did it?"

"BH Exploration Consultants."

"Chris Harper's outfit? God, that was a terrible thing, tragic. Does this have something to do with that? Are you investigating his murder?"

Stark nodded.

"I see. I don't get it, though. I thought he was killed by a burglar. What's all this—" he swept his hand over the files "have to do—"

"I don't know. Maybe it *was* a burglar. But, maybe not. Anyway, I'm a funny kind of guy. I don't like loose ends. This is a loose end. That's all." Stark said, smiling.

"Hmm. Well, is there anything else? I got to try to educate some of these little buggers. All they want to do these days is play with god-damned computers. Is that it?"

"Yeah, that's terrific, Professor Thomas."

"Call me Tim. The teenagers call me Tim, disrespectful little twits, so why shouldn't a grownup and a friend of Charlie Hayden's call me Tim?"

"Why not? Thanks, Tim."

"You're welcome. Say, could you leave me a couple of those Frenchie cigarettes—"

****

Chilly was hot when Stark got him out of the holding cells at 52 Division. Chilly had no record, beyond a couple of causing-a-disturbance offences some years before, so Stark knew that the judge would release him on his own recognizance, so Stark had called the officers on the credit card case and asked them to re-arrest Chilly right after his court appearance on the murder charge. Chilly was shaking even more than usual when Stark showed up, and Stark knew it wasn't entirely from the cold, and that's what he was counting on.

"You had no right to do that, lockin' me up like that. I didn't kill nobody. I didn't steal those credit cards, either. I found a wallet, is all. Okay, maybe I'm wrong about the salvage bit, maybe I shouldn't have sold the credit cards to that druggie, but I didn't know. I wasn't tryin' to do nuthin' wrong. It's not like I was tryin' to break the law. Maybe it just happened. But then you throw me in the god-damned dungeon again, like I'm a—pervert or somethin'.''

"Chilly, you're a suspect in a murder, for God's sake."

"I ain't done no murder. I told you that. Didn't I tell you that?"

"Yeah, you told me that. Now I want you to tell me something else. I want you to tell me the truth."

"I told you the truth."

"No, you didn't, Chilly. But you're going to, aren't you?"

"What are you goin' to do, hit me with a rubber hose, or somethin'?"

"No rubber hose, Chilly. Look, it's very simple. In the trunk of my car, I've got three nice bottles of ruby port wine." Chilly's eyebrows lifted. "As soon as you tell me the truth, Chilly—and I promise you, I will know when you're telling the truth—as soon as you tell me the truth, you can have those bottles, Chilly, and a nice big old down-filled coat with a parka that I got out of my closet especially for you—and a blanket. You can have all of that, Chilly, when you tell me the truth."

Chilly rubbed his chin thoughtfully. Finally, he said: "Okay, okay, I'll tell you, but only if you promise you'll forget about this damned murder thing."

"Chilly, if you tell me you killed somebody, then the murder charge will have to proceed. If you tell me you robbed somebody—then I might have to charge you with that. But chances are pretty good, I would guess, that I can drop the murder charge, Chilly. But I can guarantee you that if you don't tell me the truth, I'll let the murder charge stand, and they'll lock you up in the Don Jail."

"Okay, okay, I'll tell you. I'll tell you exactly what happened."

"Good."

"Umm." Chilly grinned. "We should go down to the car—because we gotta go in the car, so's I can show you, because—"

"All right, Chilly. Let's go."

Chilly directed Stark to an alley south of Wellesley Street and west of Church, right behind a club called The Purple that Stark knew was a gay bar. The sun was gleaming bright but offered no warmth against what was a frigid day, and both Stark and Chilly were rubbing their arms to ward off the cold. Chilly pointed to a spot on the pavement, and said, "Right there, that's where I found it."

Stark shook his head. He grabbed Chilly by the upper arm and began pulling him toward the car. "C'mon, Chilly, let's go—"

"No, wait, wait. I'm goin' to tell ya."

"Tell!"

"They was two of 'em. A big guy, kind of pudgy, and a small guy, and they was havin' an argumint about somethin'. I dunno what. And then the big guy grabs the little guy and sort of shakes him, and the little guy—he was pissed, eh, so he was havin' trouble standing, and he kind of stumbled and fell down, and that's when I—that's when I noticed that there was this wallet lyin' there on the ground—you know right near where he was lyin'."

"Lyin' is right. The wallet came out of his pocket, didn't it, Chilly?"

"You said you wasn't—"

"I'm not going to charge you, Chilly. Did it come out of his pocket?"

"I guess it did, yeah."

"And then what happened?"

"Nothin' really. The big guy picked the other guy up and dusted him off and they left. I didn't pay no attention to them after that."

"You were more interested in the wallet?"

Chilly shrugged.

"When they were having this argument—"

"Yeah?"

"By the way, when was this, what day was it?"

Chilly made his twisted face even more contorted in thought. "I'm sorry, Cap'n, I can't remember. I don't know nothin' about days, you know. They's all the same to me."

"Okay, these two men. Did you hear what they said? And listen, Chilly, this is where your answer really counts for you. Either you remember really well—and don't make stuff up, or I'll know—and you know what'll happen then."

Chilly muttered something under his breath. Then he studied the pavement as if it might have recorded the men's words. After a moment he nodded.

"Okay. I got it now. I was just tryin' to put it all in order, eh, know what I mean? Okay, so the first thing I remember what the big guy said is sumpin' like: 'Forget this thing,' or this idea, or somethin' like that. 'Just let it ride and it'll be okay, just don't do nothin', or somethin' like that. And then the little guy, he says, 'What are you so worried about? They ain't goin' to do nothin' to us. And if you're so worried, we'll just do a leak on the—stuff'—on the results, that's what he said, on the results. 'We'll do a leak on the results. And they won't be able to prove it was us what did it.'

"He said that, I remember." Chilly nodded, pleased with himself. "And then the big guy—oh yeah, that's right—the big guy, he gets all excited and he grabs the little guy and he says: 'Don't be stupid. These guys don't give a shit about proof' I remember he said that for sure. 'These guys is killers' I sure remember that. 'These guys will fuckin' kill us' And he said the word 'fuckin', I'm telling you that, Cap'n. 'These guys will fuckin' kill us,' that's what he said, and then he shook the other guy and the other guy, the little guy, he fell down. And then they didn't say nothin' after that, except, you know, like 'get up' and 'let's go,' and shit like that. That's it, that's all, that's everythin', Cap'n. Can I go now?"

Stark was distracted, thinking. He lit a cigarette. Chilly was looking up at him, submissively stooped, grinning pathetically, his head on one side, pleading "Eh Cap'n, can I, can we, uh—" He jerked his head in the direction of the car trunk. Finally Stark came out of his reflections.

"Eh? Okay, Chilly. You can go. Get the fuck out of here."

"Oh say, Cap'n—uh—" Chilly nodded toward the trunk again.

"What? Oh that. That was a bit of a fib, Chilly. Chilly's face dropped. "Don't worry about it. Here—here's twenty bucks, Chilly. That way you can pick your own poison, ok?"

"Oh that's great, Cap'n. Very generous, very nice. I thank you fer that."

"There's one other thing, Chilly, and this is very important. These two men, would you recognize them again? If you saw them?"

Chilly rubbed his chin thoughtfully with one hand, fingering the twenty with the other. "Yeah," he said at last, "I think I could. It was kinda dark, but I think I could. Say, supposin' I remember somethin' else—"

"You'd better remember everything right now, Chilly. Don't fuck with me."

"No, no, that's okay, Cap'n, twenty bucks is great. That's all I remember. You're right, Cap'n, that's all I remember." Chilly scuttled away up the alley. Stark called after him, "Chilly." Chilly turned his head, but kept moving. "I'm going to send somebody to find you later, get you to identify somebody. Okay?"

"That'll be fine, Cap'n. That'll be fine," Chilly said, with a wave of his hand.

Stark watched him go and shook his head. Later, he remembered he'd forgotten to give Chilly the coat.

Chapter Twelve

Later in the afternoon, Stark sat discreetly in the back corner of the funeral home chapel. The place smelled like dead flowers. It was oppressively hot. A hidden speaker piped out dolorous organ music. The casket was closed. One of the undertakers officiated. No representative of any organized religion was present.

In the hall outside the chapel, Stark had heard a woman in her late fifties talking to a man and a woman of about the same age. He figured the single woman was Harper's mother and the couple the Johnsons' parents, and based on where they were now sitting, he figured he'd been right. The lone woman had expressed annoyance that the funeral would have no religious component. "He was raised as a Presbyterian. Went to Sunday school. These young people think it's smart not to go to church, but at a time like this—"

"Apparently, this was his wish, Mildred," the man said. "That's what Dianne told us. She still goes to church, you know, Catholic, of course, but I'm sure she'd have been happy to have a Presbyterian minister here, but she wanted to honour Chris's wishes."

A series of friends stood in turn at the lectern and offered eulogies. They included some of the people Stark had interviewed. Some of the paeans were written, some not. The written ones all had the quality of academic dissertations and sounded as if they were referring to an historical figure and not a real person, someone they knew about, not someone they knew.

One young woman read a terrible poem she had written, for which several people congratulated her later. Bishop took his turn, but managed to get only a few words out before being overcome by tears. Stark noticed another man, in the corner opposite his, who was also crying, crying quietly—more sorrowfully, it appeared to Stark, than mournfully.

There was to be no cemetery service. Harper would be cremated. Stark stood in the hall outside the chapel, waiting for the person he wanted to speak to. Dianne Johnson spotted him and came over. Stark said his condolences, which she received with a nod.

"I'd like to move back into my apartment. Is it all right if I do that? I can't possibly see why—"

"I'm sorry—not yet."

Johnson started to say something, and then sighed instead. She began to turn away. Stark touched her arm.

"I'm sorry, I wasn't going to bother you, but there is one small thing. In the days before your husband died, did you see him with his wallet?"

"His wallet?"

"The missing wallet."

She shook her head as if puzzled or irritated by the question. "No, I—I don't remember. I don't understand."

"Well, it's nothing. Just a—once again, I'm sorry, but there is one other thing."

She sighed. "What?"

"When you were locked in the closet—"

"What about it?"

"I was just wondering why you didn't escape through the trap door."

She looked puzzled. "Trap door? What are you talking about?"

"In the pantry. The trap door in the pantry."

"What trap door in the pantry? What are you *talking* about? There's no trap door in the pantry. Trap door to where? There's another apartment below ours. You're not making any sense."

Stark stared at her. She was either a bloody good liar or she really didn't know about the door. Finally he said, "There *is* a trap door, Mrs—Ms Johnson. There's an old flight of stairs beneath it that leads to a concealed entrance in the ground floor foyer. They were for the use of the servants when it was all one big house. You didn't know about it?"

"I certainly didn't. Now, if you don't mind—" She turned, and her sister took her by the elbow, glared at Stark and led her into the crowd of friends and relatives.

Stark stood there, gazing into space. He almost missed the man he wanted to speak to, remembering to look for him only just in time. The man was rounding a corner leading to the exit. Stark hurried after him, caught up with him in the parking lot.

"Mr Bishop."

Bishop stopped short and turned quickly, surprised to see Stark.

"Detective Stark, I didn't see you in there. Very sad. Nice service, though, don't you think? All his friends. He was so well-liked. Nice of you to come."

Stark nodded. "Mr Bishop—"

"Yes. Is there—is there something? Have you found the, uh—the killer?"

"I noticed you were quite emotional in there. You and Harper were very close."

119

"Very close, yes. I think I told you that."

"You did, yes."

"Listen, I'm sorry, Mr Stark, but I am rather disturbed by all this, and I was just on my way home. If there's nothing—"

"Well, Mr Bishop, actually there is something. I just wanted to say that if there's anything that you might have thought of, or might think of that would help me in my investigation—"

"I told you before, Stark, that—"

"I wanted to say that you should feel free to call me at any time. Perhaps there's something that might strike you, something that was bothering you, and you might want to tell me about it, and what I want to do is to give you every opportunity to be as helpful as you can be, in order to avoid any—difficulties."

"What difficulties?"

"This morning, a gentleman—a homeless person, in fact—told me about something he had observed in an alleyway more than a week ago involving two people who had an argument. In fact, he heard the details of the argument, which he related to me. This argument got a little physical, and one of the parties actually fell to the ground at one point. Now, this homeless gentleman can identify the parties involved, and, if I have to, I will enlist his aid and have him do exactly that. And that, Mr Bishop, is all I wanted to tell you. I just wanted to keep you up to date with the latest developments in the case. That's all."

Bishop's expression revealed nothing that suggested he'd been disturbed by Stark's words. He looked, instead, as if he'd been confronted with someone irrational. "Mr Stark, I don't know for the life of me what you're telling me this for or what the hell you're talking about. You seem to be speaking in riddles. But if that's what you wanted to tell me, then consider I've been told. Now, if you don't mind—"

"Yes, you carry on, Mr Bishop. I will be seeing you." Stark thought he noticed Bishop twitch slightly at the promise of a future encounter.

****

Stark went from the funeral to Carbo's, where he downed several Scotches. He realized the evening would come to a premature halt if he kept up that pace, so he left Carbo's and walked along Queen, all the way down to an Italian restaurant near the streetcar loop, where he ate a veal dish and drank coffee.

Then he walked through the grounds of the waterworks, and stood for ten minutes staring at the lake. When the cold began to eat into his bones, he jogged back out to the street, hailed a cab and went home.

Powder, his long-haired white cat that spent most of its time curled up in a closet, had decided to make an appearance, and mewed and rubbed against his legs until he fed her. He switched on the TV, heard some young reporter butcher the language and turned it off in disgust. He turned on a Betty Carter CD—her London concert, made instant coffee in an oversized thermal mug, and sat at the kitchen table, smoking Gauloises.

The cat rubbed against his legs again and he knew she wanted water. He used to tell people his cat had a drinking problem, because she would drink water only two ways: from the faucet in the bathtub, adjusted so it drizzled in a thin stream, or by dipping one paw in a bowl and licking the water from the paw.

The water was still dripping when he awoke, still

sitting at the kitchen table, his neck aching from having been tilted to one side, his mouth dust dry from having been hung open to the elements, his nose stuffed and his head aching. He turned off the tap. The cat had retreated to the closet. He abandoned the idea of going back to Carbo's, poured himself a Scotch, downed it, stretched out on the couch, switched on the TV and fell immediately asleep. In a few moments, he woke up, soaked with perspiration. He'd had the dream. He swung his legs to floor and sat, covering his eyes with his hands.

Chapter Thirteen

The face was a bloody pulp, smashed beyond recognition, every bone shattered. There was no identification on the body, nothing but a tattered leather wallet, empty except for a brittle, yellowed letter addressed to "Horace" and signed "Mum." If Booger hadn't happened along in the alley off Wellesley Street, they might never have known that this was Chilly.

The beat cop who found him was an old-timer. He knew Stark and he knew Stark had interviewed Chilly, though he didn't know why. On his own hook, he called Stark directly. The call woke the detective.

"Sarge, it's John Tilman. Remember me?"

Stark was lousy with names. He didn't remember Tilman's. He'd hardly heard what Tilman had said. It had been a rumbling noise on top of a buzzing in his head. The rumbling stopped; the buzzing wouldn't—until he reached out and fisted the button on his clock radio. At some point in the night, he must have staggered into bed. He didn't remember. "What did you say—Tilman?" (His unconscious mind replayed the rumbling a little clearer, but the only thing discernible was "Tilman.") "Yes, Mr Tilman, what can I do for you?"

"It's John Tilman. Remember, we worked together on the Cassidy case. Last time I saw you was at Solly Firman's funeral. We got pissed at the Legion—argued about capital punishment."

"Oh, John, I'm sorry, yeah." (He still didn't remember). "What's happening, John?"

"I'm down here at a phone booth on Wellesley. There's a wino in an alley near here who's very dead. I think he's the guy you were talking to the other day."

"Oh, Christ, no. Not Chilly. Oh, my God, no."

"Yeah, that's what the other rubby called him. I figured you'd be interested, so I called you first. Some of those other assholes have got it in for you. They might just file the thing, and not even tell you about it. So I called you first. I haven't even called it in yet. I can give you ten minutes, then I gotta call it in, but that'll give you time to get here. They ain't goin' to move fast for a wino."

Stark sighed. "Thanks—John. I'll be right there."

Tilman had been right. Stark got there even before the coroner. It was the same alley, in the same spot that Chilly had taken him to. Chilly was in a corner formed by two offset buildings on the opposite side of the alley from the rear of The Purple. The back of his head was propped up in the corner, his body stretched out, legs apart, feet flopped to either side. What had been his face was chopped meat. There was a dark patch of congealed blood on his chest, like a bib. He was wearing black polyester trousers with a silver fleck and a brown work shirt with "Fred" in an oval on the breast pocket. Long, dark streaks in the crust of snow and ice on the pavement showed that he'd been dragged from a jumble of blankets and newspapers and cardboard against another wall a few feet away. Stark and Tilman and Booger stood looking at the body, their shoulders hunched down in their coats against the cold, like an unlikely trio at a graveside. The wind was swirling a light sprinkle of snow into a vortex that spun around them.

Through his tears, Booger told Stark that that was Chilly's place.

"Chilly slept here, in this kind of weather?" Stark said, stamping his feet. "He was cold indoors, for Christ's sake."

"Chilly didn't like it in them shelters. They's too rough, too many punks. Either that or they tells ya what to do. Chilly didn't like that. So he'd get all wrapped up, like one of them cackoons, under all them blankets and the cardboard. And he stuffed newspaper into his coat. He got a new coat just last week from the Sally Ann, leather, real long one, almost to yer ankles. He hid it under the cardboard, days. Only wore it nights. Somebody might steal it."

"He's not wearing it now."

"Somebody must have tooken it."

"You mean whoever killed him took his coat? They killed him for his leather coat?"

Booger made a face that acknowledged the possibility, but said, "Thing is, you wouldn't know he had the coat, because he'd be all wrapped up. Only wore it, you know, when he was sleepin'—under everythin' like. More likely somebody came along and saw him lyin' there—" he pointed to the body, "—and took the coat off him. Figured he wouldn't need it no more. That's more like."

Stark shook his head.

"Okay—Booger, is it?"

"That's what they call me—on account of—"

Stark put his hand up. "That's okay, Booger. I don't—. You hang around here?"

"Not this kind of weather. I'm at the Love of Life

Mission most nights. Just around in the daytime. Used to be here with Chilly most of the time. Him and me was great pals." He started to cry again. "Funny thing, ain't it? Chilly hated the cold, but he stayed outdoors winter and summer. Me, I don't mind it so much, but I always goes indoors winters."

"Well, thanks, Booger. You can go." Tilman looked at Stark, puzzled that he was letting Booger leave without asking him more questions.

"Mind if I stick around until they takes him away? I'd sort of like to see him off, ya know?"

"Sure. Just stay back out of the way, though, will you?"

The coroner's wagon pulled into the alley. Stark moved out of the way, looking around for windows that might have offered a view of the alley. When he turned back, he saw the coroner from behind, young woman who, Stark thought, had a nice way of bending over the body. He asked her how long Chilly had been dead and what kind of weapon had killed him.

"For God's sake, give me a second, will you?" She had a voice like rusty razor blades and a face to match. Stark averted his gaze, rolling his eyes.

After a time, she said, "I'd say not less than six hours, not more than ten. Looks like a baseball bat or something similar. Could be a length of pipe."

"Thanks." Stark turned to Tilman—he'd already forgotten the name again. He had remembered the constable's face when he saw it, but he couldn't remember drinking with him in a Legion hall. "You heard?"

"Gotcha. We're looking for a baseball bat or a piece of wood like it, or a lead pipe. Okay, I'll organize that,

Sarge."

"Thanks."

"Your Homicide boys still ain't here."

"No. I called them, told them I'd take it."

"Oh. Okay. I'll get the search goin'."

"And you'd better knock on some doors around here. See if anybody was here late, see if anybody lives in any of these windows up there. Talk to passing winos. You know what to do."

"I'll take care of it, Sarge."

In the end, they found no weapon and no witnesses.

****

Stark buzzed Bishop's apartment. He thought he heard a click on the speaker, as if somebody had pushed the button to speak, but it was followed by silence. There was a security camera in the corner of the foyer's ceiling. Bishop could be watching him. He had to be home. The answering service girl had recognized Stark's voice. This time she was excited at talking to a detective, and she liked to talk. "He's at home, Mr Stark, and he sounded awful, very ill. Said he wouldn't be back at work until next week, and that he would let me know, and that I was to take messages and tell people he was out of town. Of course, I know you're not, you know, an ordinary person. I have to tell you the truth when you ask me, don't I?"

"That's the best idea, yes."

"Well, then he's at home, Mr Stark. Do you have the address?"

Stark did, and he found it encouraging that Bishop didn't want to see him. There was a sign beside the bank of apartment buzzer buttons: The Surrey Manor Management Office, and a phone number. Stark went out to his car, and used his cell phone to call the number.

127

A woman answered in a bored voice, as if she was tired of hearing complaints. Stark told her who he was, and asked her to meet him in the lobby. She demanded to know what it was about, and he told her in an icy voice that it was none of her god-damned business, and that she'd better be waiting for him in the thirty seconds it would take him to get to the apartment entrance or he'd kick the god-damned door in. She was there waiting for him, glaring, a tiny woman in her thirties wearing a shapeless blue suit. She had tight lips and a little, pointed nose. She let him in.

"I'm going to report you. Using language like that."

He ignored her. "I want you to open apartment four-one-one for me."

"I can't do that. Not without the occupant's permission. This is a condominium, you know. These are all private residences."

"But you have a master key?"

"Yes, for safety reasons. I have to have a master key, or if the lock is changed, I have to have a copy of the key, but I still can't—"

"You want me to kick the door in."

She blustered. "You'd better not. You'd have to have a warrant—"

"I'll get a warrant here in half an hour, and then I'll kick the door in, and in the meantime I'll have twelve police cars pull up in your driveway with their sirens going and their lights flashing. How do you think the residents are going to like that?"

"This is an outrage. All right, I'll open the door, but I'm going to put everything in writing and send it to the police commission, you understand me?"

"I understand you all right. Come on, let's go."

When they got to Bishop's door, the woman looked defiantly at Stark and knocked loudly. Stark stared back, unblinking. The woman looked away. There was no answer.

"There's no one home," she said smugly.

"Unlock it."

"I told you, I can't—"

Stark grabbed the key from her hand.

"What are you doing? You can't—" The door opened before Stark had got the key into the lock. Bishop was standing there in a housecoat, a towel around his neck, his hair wet and stringy, out of the pony tail, touching his shoulders .

"Why, Mr Stark, I don't—did you ring the buzzer? And Ms Waterford, nice to see you. Is there some problem?"

The woman's change of expression was startling. It was as if she'd put on a different face, become a different creature, shape-shifting from a yapping Chihuahua into a fawning collie, practically panting as Bishop graced her with his gaze. Stark thought he detected more than just professional deference in her manner. She touched her hair, and her pose relaxed.

"I'm so sorry, Mr Bishop, but this—man insisted that I—"

Bishop raised a hand. "Don't worry about it, Ms Waterford. Detective Stark is a friend of mine. I was in the shower. I didn't hear him buzz. He knew I was home and I suppose he got anxious. He's a very busy man," he said, shielding his mouth with his hand as if he was sharing a confidence that explained Stark's bad manners.

"I see. Well, I'll—leave you, then. If there's anything you need, Mr Bishop, you know where I am."

"Of course. Won't you come in, Detective?"

Bishop's apartment was a sharp contrast to his office. As sparse and utilitarian as his workplace was, his residence was lush and decorative, festooned with plants, arrayed with paintings, mostly abstracts in garish colours. Every available space not taken up by oversized flora was occupied by Chinese vases and statuary and other *objets d'art*. The furniture was overstuffed and overpillowed and richly upholstered. On one wall of the living room, there was a phalanx of mirrors of various shapes and sizes, some of them convex, so that Stark saw himself and Bishop reflected and distorted.

Bishop indicated that Stark should take a large leather chair that was clearly the place of honour. Stark sat on the first six inches of the seat.

"Can I offer you a coffee, Mr Stark? Or would you prefer something stronger?"

"Nothing, thanks."

"Very well." Bishop sat in the corner of an immense sectional sofa that stretched twelve feet. He gathered his hair behind his neck. "What can I do for you?"

Stark stared at Bishop for a long time. Bishop smiled inanely—remarkably calm, betraying no sign of fear or curiosity. Stark noticed his eyes were a little glassy. He wondered whether Bishop had fortified himself with a mood-altering substance.

Finally, he said, "Bishop, what I have to say is short and nasty. I'm having a little trouble restraining myself right now from coming over there and slapping you silly." Bishop's smile vanished. "Two people are dead— I believe because of you, because of what you've done and what you've said."

Bishop leaned forward and opened his mouth to say

something. Stark cut him off.

"Don't bother—don't say anything. Just listen. I know all about your little Royal Cross adventure." Bishop eyelids fluttered. "I know all about Salvatore Cataldi." Stark sighed. "I made a big mistake telling you about Chilly yesterday—"

"Who?"

"I didn't give you his name, but I didn't have to, did I? You knew who he was. He's always in the same spot, right behind where you and Harper used to go on a regular basis. You knew right away who he was."

"I don't know what you're—"

"Please—Bishop, don't waste my time. After I told you your little tiff with Harper had been seen, and that Chilly could identify you—"

"Who is—Chilly?"

"— you went straight to Cataldi and told him, and you told him exactly where to find Chilly, and Cataldi said he'd take care of it, and he did, Bishop. He took care of it."

Stark looked down at the intricately patterned green-and-blue Persian rug. Bishop started to speak, but Stark held both hands up quickly and Bishop's mouth shut like a clam.

Stark said, "I don't know exactly why I came here now, Bishop. I'd like to arrest you. I would arrest you, but I haven't got enough hard evidence yet. Normally, I wouldn't warn a subject. It's not good practice, but—I guess I wanted to confess my sin of stupidity and carelessness to somebody—what I did cost a poor man his life, and, bizarrely, you're my father confessor, Bishop.

"I guess you've got the right name for it. And there's

another thing. I think you're into something way over your head, and I think you might want to take advantage of the cleansing power of the confessional yourself, to get it off your chest. I'm leaving now, and I'll let you think about it. I'm going to tell you this before I go. If you don't open up, you're going to end up like your bosom buddy Harper and like Chilly. That's it. No, don't say anything, or I might hit you. I'm going."

Stark got up and walked quickly out of the apartment. Bishop sat with one finger raised and his mouth agape, but Stark had closed the door before Bishop could think of something to say.

Chapter Fourteen

To call Cataldi Enterprises unassuming would be understating the case. The face it presented to the world was of plate glass, lined with tightly shut vertical blinds in a converted dry-cleaning shop at the end of a small strip mall in Woodbridge, north of Toronto. Its closest neighbours were a bakery, a video rental chain outlet and a convenience store. Stark parked at the opposite end of the lot from Cataldi's, far enough along that he was past the line of sight of the convenience store.

He played jazz CDs and waited. He waited because he knew he had no solid reason for being there, knew that he was probably going to accomplish nothing. He'd hit a dead end. He'd convinced himself that Cataldi's people were the killers. The slug on the back of his head brought them right into the centre of it. But there was nothing in his investigation of the crimes to point directly to them. No physical evidence. No witnesses. Merely a tenuous circumstantial connection.

And unless Bishop caved in, Stark could think of no way to make the link firm. And even if Bishop did collapse—and he doubted he would—he'd probably go down alone. Bishop was terrified of these people. What Chilly had heard in the alley made that clear.

So Stark knew that, realistically, the chances of nailing them were practically nil. And if he couldn't nail them, he couldn't implicate Bishop in a conspiracy, which is what he really wanted to do.

No. Bishop wouldn't talk. He was too frightened to talk, and there was no percentage in it. Stark couldn't pin the killings on him. If he could, he would have arrested him already. That's what he should have done. Warning him was a mistake. He'd already told Bishop he had a motive. There was no more concrete evidence he was going to be able to gather—nothing that was going to put Bishop at the scene of the crime, and he doubted he'd been there anyway. Although he must have pointed out Chilly to them, but perhaps not—he knew where Chilly holed up, knew that Chilly slept there.

No. If Cataldi's boys had done the deed, which had to be—it had to be them—then Bishop hadn't been there. If Bishop had been there, how was Stark going to prove it, anyway? If he could have, he would have, and he'd have arrested Bishop. So that's why he was here to see Cataldi, he reminded himself—to try something off the wall, something desperate, to try to foment a little dissension in the ranks. Threaten the bastards. Stir up shit. Make something happen. At least he'd have the satisfaction of letting the scum know that he knew they'd done it.

It was brilliantly sunny day. The little shopping mall was at the intersection of Highway 7 and a north-south regional road.

It sat halfway up a hill, affording a broad panorama off to the west of rolling, snow-covered hills glinting in the sun and dotted with massive homes, many of which, Stark knew, had mailboxes at the roadside that were lettered with names like Crupi and Fanti and Santoro, nice, hard-working people who had nothing to do with the likes of Cataldi. But a smattering of the mailboxes, in this predominantly Italian area, he knew, would belong to people who would have dealings with Cataldi and his fellow-travellers.

There was a gas station kitty-cornered, and he watched a big fuel truck come in, and the driver withdraw the long dipstick from the filler hole and check it before attaching the hose and pumping in more gasoline, putting back in the ground what had been drawn out of the ground halfway across the country, and which Stark was going to have pumped out of the ground again before he left the area, since he was just about out of gas.

At the corner of his eye, he caught a movement in a white field a long way off. When he focused on it, he saw two horses prancing and fencing with each other. "Horsing around," he thought, "which is just about what I'm doing."

He opened the car door and caught a surprising blast of frigid air in the face. He grimaced and then, shaking his head, smiled at the thought that no matter how long you live in this country, when you look at the outdoors—especially on a sunny day—through glass from a warm place and then go outside, you're always shocked by the fact that it's bloody cold out there.

He stood beside the car, stretched, stamped his feet and automatically checked to see that the gun he didn't think he'd ever be able to draw again was in place. Then he put his collar up, hunched his shoulders against the wind and trotted across the parking lot to the door of Cataldi Enterprises.

A small glass-and-aluminum entranceway had been added to the front of the building to keep the weather out when you opened the door to the office. The inner door, covered with opaque material, was locked. There was a video camera in the upper corner and a buzzer button beside the door. He pressed the button and waited—

perhaps ten seconds. There was a click and the door popped off the latch. He pushed it open and went in to face a counter that had been installed when the place was a dry cleaners. You could see a faint outline of the letters "Supreme Cleaners" across the front of the counter. A young woman with a mass of blonde curls and pink lips looked at him blankly with eyes that might have been outlined with a felt-tipped pen.

"Can I help you?" she said as if she had no interest in the answer, her voice sounding like guitar strings snapping in a steel garbage can.

"Yeah, I'd like to see—"

"Detective Stark, I believe it is, am I right?" Stark's head inclined toward the receptionist, but his eyes moved to gaze in the direction of the voice.

The speaker was a short young man, finely featured, too good-looking and so perfectly turned out that he looked almost gaudy. Stark barely succeeded in concealing his surprise at being on this swine's list of known persons. The surprise vanished with the obvious explanation for his being recognized. Standing beside the man who was obviously Salvatore Cataldi was a creature built like a boxcar and an expression that suggested he had brains to match.

Stark made a rapid scan of the room. There were six pigeon-hole, glass-walled offices—three on each side, and only two occupied—the one Cataldi had emerged from and another in which someone was bent over a computer; a small man with a pony tail and a triangular bald patch on the back of his head.

"I assume you're Cataldi."

Cataldi's cheek gave a tiny twitch. "Might be nicer if you called me *Mr* Cataldi, but then, why stand on ceremony. In fact, Sal will be fine. And you, you're Harry, I believe. Come on in, Harry. Marie, open the gate for the officer, please."

Marie gave Cataldi a puzzled look, as if inviting a policeman into the inner sanctum was not something she would have expected her employer to do. Then she shrugged and pressed a button that released the catch on a gate at one end of the counter. Stark went in and followed Cataldi's gesture to join him in his office.

"Take a pew, Harry," Cataldi said, indicating a cheap chrome-and-vinyl, armless office chair in a corner. The chair matched the rest of the furnishings in the office in its age and lack of quality, but matched nothing in the office in style or appearance. In fact, nothing seemed to match anything else and all of it looked as if it had been bought at one of those second-hand warehouses in Scarborough.

There was a temporary, thrown-together look about the place. Sagging cardboard boxes filled with brochures and paper were stacked all over and had a dusty, untouched look, which, together with the empty offices, suggested that business was not booming. At the time, the real estate market was in a big slump.

"So what can I do for you, Harry? You're a long way out of your bailiwick. You on loan to the OPP, or something? Somebody bump somebody off in the corner store? I hadn't heard anything—but then I don't get around much. I hardly ever get out of this place, and my associates are almost never out of my sight." He smiled thinly.

"That's funny, because I've met your associates, but I didn't see you there. Of course, maybe you were in another room, calling your broker to buy some more stock in Delsim Mining. Is that possible?"

Stark thought he saw a slight movement of Cataldi's

body at the mention of Delsim. Cataldi grinned. "Anything, my father used to say, is possible except two hills without a valley and a clock that strikes less than one. But, in this instance, I don't know what you're talking about. You say you've met my associates. Where might that have been?" Cataldi picked up a letter opener and absently worked it under one perfectly manicured, immaculate fingernail.

"I'm not going to piss around, Cataldi. Your goons here will have told you about me. How else would you know my bloody name? They'll have told you I can't identify them. Even the one with the funny bald spot and the ridiculous pony tail. Of course I could lie and say I saw their faces, but that wouldn't be playing the game: at least, not according to my rules. That would make me no better than you, Cataldi, and then the good guys wouldn't win, only a different kind of bad guy."

"Very philosophical, Harry. I'm impressed with your high moral fibre—not pleased, on the other hand, with your implied characterization of me, but impressed, nonetheless. The reason I know you is because I saw your face on television the other day. They said you were the lead investigator in some killing. They tried to speak to you in fact. You don't speak much to the media, do you?" He smiled briefly and then his expression hardened. He leaned toward Stark. "You say you don't want to piss around. Okay, neither do I. I haven't got time for games. I'm a busy man."

Stark looked around. "Yeah, I can see that."

"What the hell do you want, Stark? Why'd you come all the way out here to bother me? Or was it just for that— to bother me?"

Stark stared hard at Cataldi. He despised this slick little man sitting opposite him, despised him not only for what he stood for and what he did, but for his glib manner and arrogance, despised him because he valued things and people alike as commodities, some worth more, some less, some nothing to him. Stark despised him because Cataldi's side was winning.

Strangely, it also bothered Stark that he despised this man, bothered him because he had long since given up hatred as a waste of time and energy, something that screwed up your head, caused you to make mistakes. Stark was good at what he did in large part *because* he had given up hatred. He didn't hate the killers he caught and prosecuted, no matter how brutal their crimes had been. Retribution was not his business. Catching criminals was. And he knew he'd never catch Cataldi. Probably that's what bothered him most of all.

"At the risk of offending you with a cliché, Cataldi, I'm going to lay my cards on the table."

"Yes, that isn't very original, but lay away."

"And please don't interrupt me with any pointless protests." Cataldi shrugged. "I know you killed, or had killed, two men, Chris Harper and Horace MacIver." Cataldi screwed up his face. "No, you don't know him as Horace MacIver. You probably don't know him as anything. They called him Chilly, a poor, useless wino who lived in an alley and didn't bother anybody. But he saw something he shouldn't, so you had him killed."

Cataldi shook his head. Stark put his hand up. "I told you. Don't bother denying this stuff. It's a waste of time. Besides, I can't prove that you did either of these crimes—not now, and probably not ever. But you never know. You never know. Anyway, here's what I want. I know all about you and Delsim and Shane Bishop. I can't have you—maybe—but I promise you I'll make your life a hell if you don't co-operate. What I want, because I *can* have *him,* and because—well, I *want* him. I want you to give him up to me—Bishop."

Cataldi laughed.

"I'm serious, Cataldi. You want the heat off you, put it on Bishop. I don't know how you can give him up, but I'm sure you can think of something—imaginative. I'm sure you've got a wonderful imagination, Cataldi. So—do it. I'm giving you five days."

Cataldi gave him a forced look of disbelief, and finally said, "I think you've lost it, Stark. You've snapped. You're nuts. You're talking about a whole bunch of people I've never heard of. I don't know this Bishop guy, and we don't kill people, Stark. At the risk of offending *you* with a cliché, I'd say you've been reading too many cheap detective novels. What is it, because I've got an Italian name? Why *did* you pick me, anyway? You're really crazy. Now, I want you to get the hell out of my office and fast, because if you don't, I'm going to call my friend on the police commission and report you for harassing an innocent businessman. I'm going to report you for bigotry. Now get the fuck out."

Stark shook his head. "You know, the biggest cliché is your righteous indignation. It's almost embarrassing."

"You're the only embarrassing thing around here, Stark. You're an embarrassment to the police force. You've gone past the 'best-before' date. You ought to retire, Stark. You really should. You're so far off base, you're in a different god-damned sport. Now—would you leave?—please."

Stark sat in his car in the parking lot for some time, thinking about what Cataldi had said. Maybe he was right. Maybe he *was* past it. This was his first case after the shooting. He'd thrown himself into it—desperately, maybe so desperately that he was being irrational.

Chapter Fifteen

Coroner Marv Greenberg was in Florida. Stark had forgotten to ask the name of the female coroner who'd attended to Chilly. He tried to describe her to the switchboard operator at the Centre of Forensic Sciences, but he could hardly say, "She had a voice like rusty razor blades." Finally, after he had stumbled around for a while, the operator asked impatiently, "What's the name of the deceased?"

"Oh. Uh, Chilly. I mean MacIver, Horace MacIver. He was killed—"

"Just a minute."

The line went silent, and then after about thirty seconds, a female voice answered, "Connors. Who's speaking, please?"

"Connors? I'm sorry, Connors who? Who Connors?"

"Who is this?"

"This is Detective Harry Stark, Homicide squad. Who's this?"

"This is Coroner Cheryl Connors. What do you want, Detective?"

Her voice reminded him that he should stop trying to picture her.

"Uh, *Mizz* Connors, I wanted to get hold of Marv Greenberg."

"He's on vacation."

"I understand that. It was just because—well, I thought he might have an overview—"

"Overview?"

"Yeah. You see, I'm investigating two murders—the one you attended."

"Which one is that?"

"Horace MacIver. In the alley near Church Street, behind the—"

"I recall. What's the other murder?"

"Chris Harper. It was in the Beaches a couple of weeks ago. Marv attended."

"You think there's a connection?"

"Well, that's what I want to know. I want to know whether the same weapon could have killed both of them. Whether it could have been the same killer."

"I'm not familiar with the other case. I'll have to check the records, and call you back. Where can I reach you?"

He gave her the number and she hung up. Fifteen minutes later, she called back.

"Detective Stark?"

"Yep."

"You know I wouldn't have to be doing this if you had been at the autopsy as you were supposed to have been, as the lead investigator."

"I couldn't be there. That's why I delegated the other officer." Stark was referring to Tilman, but he'd forgotten his name again. If Tilman had made no impression on Stark the first time they'd met, Stark had certainly made an impression on the constable. When Stark had asked him whether he'd mind attending the autopsy on Chilly, Tilman had enthusiastically agreed, said he'd be delighted.

143

The woman made a snorting noise.

"Well, why didn't you ask him?" she said.

"Look—"

"Never mind. The answer is no."

"No?"

"No."

"No to what?"

"It wasn't the same weapon. In the Harper killing, the weapon was something quite wide and presumably heavy. One blow was delivered. The fractures and contusions are different. Also, the nature of the delivery is different. In the Harper killing, it was as if the intention was to kill quickly and efficiently, to be done with it. MacIver is entirely different. Since you haven't been in touch with me, you don't know the details, unless you asked somebody else here—"

"No, I haven't—"

"Well, the attack on MacIver was particularly brutal. It wasn't just his face that was struck. Both his arms and legs were broken—compound fractures—and I suspect before he was hit in the head. Whoever attacked him smashed his legs and his arms first and then struck him repeatedly in the face and the side of the head. A right-handed person, incidentally. Someone attacked him with real fury, someone who wanted to inflict pain as well as cause death. Not the same sort of killing at all. I would say it was two different people."

"Or somebody who wanted to make it look like two different people."

"I suppose that's possible."

"Yeah, anything's possible except two hills without—Jesus Christ, why am I quoting that sonofabitch?"

"What?"

"Never mind. Thanks for your help, Ms Connors."

"Call me Cheryl," she said brightly. "I'm sure we'll be working together in the future. I've heard about you. I just moved over from Hamilton. More action here."

"Yeah. Cheryl, thanks again."

As soon as he put the phone down, it rang again. The voice on the other end spoke in a whisper.

"Detective Stark?"

"That's right."

"Your office forwarded the call. I hope I'm not bothering you at home, or anything, but I had to talk to you? They told me you are the one who is investigating the murder of that man Chris Harper?"

"Who's calling?"

"My name is Jones, Doreen Jones." Her voice went up at the end of her sentences, as if everything she said was a question. "I—don't want to get involved in this, but—well, it's about my boss?"

"And who might that be?"

"Bill Bream?" This time it was a real question, as if she thought Stark might already know it.

"I'm sorry, I don't—oh, Bream. Delsim Mining."

"That's right. He's the president?"

"What about him?"

"Well, he's—there's something, something wrong. He's—oh, I don't know. He's frightened. He's not the same as he usually his? Something—he's been scared for a while now, and then when this Harper fellow got killed, I saw him read the story in the paper and he went white as a sheet. He was actually shaking? And then I—I can't talk loud because he's in the next office. The door's closed, but—"

145

"Uh, Miss—"

"Jones."

"Yeah, Miss Jones, you're saying that he, your boss, was particularly bothered by the death of Chris Harper?"

"Exactly."

"And why do you think this might have been?"

"Well—you see, I didn't know this Mr Harper. I've never met him. But I recognized the name of the company he worked for, BH Explorations?"

"Mmm."

"Because we used them on a site in Papua New Guinea. And that was kind of strange. Because they charge a lot of money. And I know we can't afford it, but we used them anyway. And—here's how it happened. They made an appointment to see Bill and then they came in to the office."

"They? Who were they?"

"I don't know. One man was called Bishop. But the other man, I don't know. He was very well dressed, I remember that: a young man, very good looking. I'm sorry, that has nothing to do with anything, but— anyway, they spoke to Bill, Mr Bream, for about fifteen minutes and then they left and Bill was—well, he was really pleased. He told me that BH would be working for us and that they were the best there is and we'd have a good chance at hitting it big? And everything was fine, and then the stock—our stock, our shares, they started to rise? And Bill said he couldn't figure it out at first, and then he got a phone call, and I recognized the voice of the man on the other end, and it was that fellow who came in with Mr Bishop, and right after that Bill started to act really frightened. He left and went home right after the first phone call."

"The first? There were others?"

"Oh yes, two or three, and Bill got more and more frightened. And then the stock exchange called, and well—he left the door open, so I heard? They wanted to know why the stock was going up, and Bill said he didn't know. He had no information to give them, that it was a mystery to him, as well. And then he came out of the office and he just stood there, and he was sweating, and it's cold in our office, so—well, it was nerves.

"Maybe I shouldn't be telling you this, but I know that Bill, Mr Bream, is a very honest man and a very good man, and he wouldn't be involved in anything, you know, crooked. So whatever is happening is not his fault. I don't know what is happening. But it has something to do with this man's death, at least I think it does. I don't know if you can do anything, but—" The words were catching in her throat. She was crying. Stark couldn't handle a woman crying.

"You've done the right thing, Miss Jones. Now listen, don't say anything to anybody else about this, especially not your boss. I'm sure he's perfectly innocent. I'm sure he didn't do anything wrong, and I want to help him. So just, you know, stay calm, and don't say anything, all right?"

"All right. Only please, please help him. because he's such a nice man and—"

"Yeah, right. Listen, don't you worry. I'm—I'll fix it. It'll be all right."

****

Stark arranged to meet Ernie Kowalski that night. Stark had suggested Carbo's, but Kowalski had said it was his bowling night, and told him he'd see him in the coffee shop at Striker's Bowl and Billiards on Victoria

Park Avenue.

"You can smoke your filthy French cigarettes in there, he'd said. "They don't give a shit."

****

Kowalski's wrinkled collar was permanently open, his tie always askew. He had a heavy beard, so that by evening his chin was bristling. Morty Greenwood had once told Stark: "I'd like to feel that against my tender cheek—and I won't tell you which cheek." Stark had seen Kowalski only in two jackets, a grey, polyester plaid in the warm weather and a beige corduroy in the cold. He was wearing the corduroy that night, over his bowling shirt and a pair of faded jeans. He put one arm around Stark and gave him a powerful squeeze just as a woman on a nearby alley got a strike and let out a piercing squeal of delight. They both turned to look, then returned their gaze to each other.

"Little pleasures," Kowalski said without sarcasm. "Harold, how the hell are you, you old fart. You're looking terrible—as usual. What are you drinking? Who do you have to kill for a drink around here?" he said loudly. An ancient, sour-faced waitress with a mass of back-combed hair began to shuffle over. "She's coming," Kowalski said out of the side of his mouth. "She may even get here before closing time." At about eight feet from the table, she stopped. Kowalski's broad smile elicited no change of expression. The woman said nothing.

Kowalski shrugged and asked Stark, "What'll you have?"

"I don't know—a beer, I guess—Molson Export."

"Make it two." Kowalski nodded to the waitress, who turned slowly and shuffled off without acknowledging the order.

"How was your game?" Stark said.

"My what?" Kowalski said, distracted. "Sorry, I was looking to see if she was actually wearing bedroom slippers."

"And was she?"

"Bowling shoes," Kowalski said, snickering.

"They'll do the trick, I guess. Maybe she's a pro bowler who works here only so she can practise after hours. Speaking about bowling, I was asking about yours. How'd you do?"

"Ah, we lost. We always lose. Scarborough Fire Department beat us again. They've got more time to practise." He chuckled. "So, my friend, I understand you went to see the gentleman we spoke of on the telephone."

"How the hell did you—have you got surveillance on the guy?"

"Oh-ho. Our eyes are everywhere, my man." He shook his head. "I only wish. The only chance we *have* with these creeps *is* if we watch them—*all* the time, twenty-four hours a day. The *only* chance. But there's no budget for it. No, we're not watching him. It was the Mounties. And don't ask me why *they're* watching him. Those guys won't tell you a damned thing." He laughed. "They wanted to know whether we knew that a cop was paying Cataldi a visit. They'll be watching you next. Lucky coincidence for you that I got the call. I told them we knew all about it, and it wasn't any of their business."

Stark waited for the celebratory shouts of a winning team to fade before he said, "But you don't know why they're interested in Cataldi?"

"No, like I told you, everything with them is a national secret—until they want *our* help. So why *did* you go to see him?"

"It's a long story—" Stark filled him in on everything up to and including the phone call from Bream's secretary, his long account punctuated by thunderous rumbling from the alleys and the clash of falling pins. When he'd finished, he sat back and said, "So, what do you think?"

"What do I think? Hmm." He rubbed his stubbled chin. "I don't know. It's weird. Obviously Cataldi has been manipulating the stock. And the terror stuff, implied threats—Bream and Bishop both running scared—that's the way he works. This Bream guy— looks like he's just a victim. And it sounds like Bishop is in over his head."

"Yeah, I think Cataldi approached Bishop and sold him on the idea, but they didn't tell Harper because Harper was the kind of straight-arrow type who wouldn't go along with that kind of shit. And then I think Harper wised up and was going to spill the beans. I think Cataldi's goon and his computer wizard went to Harper's place and did him in, and wrote the letter—the one that was supposed to be from the wife, and left it where anybody with half a brain could find it. The letter was vague enough, they could have written it, or more likely Bishop wrote it for them and they just typed it in. Then they killed the relevant files and then the wife showed up, so they locked her away in the closet, the pantry."

Kowalski was shaking his head.

"What's the matter?"

"I don't know. It doesn't—It doesn't quite hold water."

"Wait a minute, why not? If Bishop was afraid that eventually, you know after an investigation turned up something about the Delsim thing, that he'd be Number One suspect—and then I confront Bishop at the funeral and tell him that Chilly can identify the two guys arguing behind the gay bar—sorry, Ernie."

Kowalski smiled wryly. "You're such an asshole, Harry."

"I know. Anyway, Bishop calls Cataldi and says he's worried. He's gonna get nailed. Now he can be linked to a heated argument with Harper—I mean, I told him Chilly heard everything that was said—and he knows Chilly always hangs out in the same place, because he and Harper were apparently more than just colleagues."

"What a terrible thing."

"No, but that's how he knew Chilly was always there. So he tells Cataldi and the big boy—and, Christ, he is a big boy—goes down there and smashes Chilly to kingdom come."

"No, no. No way."

"What do you mean, 'no way'?"

"I mean no way. That's not their style. It doesn't fit."

"What do you mean, it doesn't fit? They killed both of them the same way, hit them with something. There's no gunshot noise, no bullets to trace, no gun to get rid of, why not?"

"Well, in the first place it doesn't fit because Cataldi is no killer. He doesn't work that way. He's a scam artist. Anything he's involved in, he's got an edge. And in the second place, the killings are inconsistent, because *these people* kill only two ways: one, and this would be the case with Chilly—but it doesn't make any sense—if they want to make an example, to post a warning to others who might be thinking of getting out of line, then they kill painfully, brutally, hideously, and leave the body where it can be found. But who the hell would they be making a point for? Bishop? I don't think so. And Harper? That's no mob killing. One bloody blow? He could have lived. He could have talked. They don't take chances. It was too loose-endy, too uncertain.

"And they wouldn't do it themselves, anyway. They'd bring in a contractor, and you'd probably never find the body. In fact, a guy like that, they might wait till he went off in the bush somewhere and do him there, and then everybody'd think he'd gotten eaten by a fucking bear or something. And you said the coroner told you it wasn't the same person killed both parties, right?"

"What does she know? I told her, 'What if it's somebody who wants to make it look like it was two different people?' What if Bishop said, 'Look, I don't want Stark to think there's a connection. Make it look like he got killed in a fight,' or something."

"You're stretching, Harry, I'm telling ya. Cataldi is no killer."

"But look. It's got to be more than a coincidence that I tell Bishop about Chilly and right away Chilly is dead. Am I right, or am I right?"

"You could be right about that—it sounds to me like you might be—but what's wrong is that you're bringing Cataldi into it. There's a lot of money involved, okay, but if things start to get too hot, Cataldi bails out, sells his shares and still makes a bundle, and he's done nothing illegal, nothing you can nail him with." Kowalski shook his head.

"In fact, why would he sell the shares? He's not a principal in the company. He's not on the board of directors. Neither Bream nor Bishop is going to say anything. Bishop could be ruined and they're both scared shitless anyway. And how are they going to prove anything, unless they wore a wire, or there was a witness—and I don't think so. I think, maybe, after I filled you in on Cataldi, that you fixated on him. You'd like it to be him. Face it, Harry, here I am trying to tell my grandmother how to suck eggs. You've been in Homicide since the Dead Sea was on the critical list. You know in your heart this isn't a mob hit."

Stark shook his head. "I know it isn't *like* a mob hit, but—"

"Harry, if I were you, I'd forget the 'buts.' It seems to me the guy you're playing down in this is Bishop, himself, like you don't think he's capable of doing it."

Stark ran his hand through his hair. "You mean that Bishop acted alone?"

"Sure. Why not?"

Stark screwed up his face. "I don't know. I guess it's possible. I mean, I should know after all these years of doing this crap that the most unlikely people *can* be killers. But this guy is *really*—I mean *really* unlikely."

"Unlikely or not, the evidence points squarely at Bishop. Suppose he was frightened that Harper was going to turn him in. Maybe he was even going to split up the partnership, and Bishop, the way you tell it, is useless without Harper. Bishop goes from being a high-living somebody to nothing, and if you add the complication of a love affair between them—pretty volatile stuff." Kowalski raised his hands in a question, took a sip of his beer, then asked, "Did you check into insurance?"

"Christ. Not yet. How stupid!"

"Right, well, usually in these partnership deals each

of the parties has a big policy in which the other is the beneficiary, especially, I would think, in this case. So, throw that in and you've got a hell of a lot of motives for Bishop's doing in Harper."

They stared at each other for a time, then Kowalski went on: "Now, Bishop thinks he'll be a logical suspect, so he covers his face with a balaclava or whatever it was, in case he gets spotted going into the place. It's so bloody cold these days, no one would think it odd. You said the killer had to be somebody that Harper knew, because of the way he was sitting at the computer and all. Bishop takes off the balaclava when he goes inside of course, then he whacks Harper, and then—wait a second. If Harper falls on the keyboard and stays there, how the hell does Bishop write the letter that's supposed to point the finger at the wife?"

"Floppy disc."

"What?"

"He writes it at home, or in the office. They'll all have the same word-processing software. He saves it on a disc and brings it with him. Then all he has to use is the mouse. He calls up the file from the floppy, saves it to the hard drive."

"What about when you said you—I don't know anything about computers—but you said there's a list of the files just opened that shows up when you do something, so wouldn't the other file show up?"

"Sure, but you could—create three blank files— only four of them show up—and then resave the letter file, so it's the top one, and the file name from the floppy would be pushed off the list. Pretty easy."

"You know a lot about this stuff."

"Bugger all, really."

"But what about getting rid of all the files about the X-King thing? How would he do that?"

"With the mouse. He wouldn't have to use the keyboard," Stake said, lighting a Gauloise.

"Whoo." Kowalski wafted his hand in front of his face. "Boy, those things stink."

"Sorry. I'll put it out."

"Naw, don't worry about it," Kowalski smiled. "Just blow it off to the side, will ya? Okay, back to Bishop. He's no cold-blooded killer, but—imagine this—he pleads with Harper to let things ride, but Harper won't have anything to do with it. He tells him that you can't cross people like Cataldi. Harper says 'forget it.' Remember, they had this argument before—in the alley—and maybe many other times. And remember, in the alley, Bishop ended up grabbing Harper and knocking him to the ground. He's got a temper and he's capable of violence. This time, he goes all the way. And you see, whoever killed Harper was no—brute. The way he was killed shows that—one blow, get it over with, one big bloody blow. Smash. So whatever he uses for a weapon—you've got no weapon, right?"

Stark shook his head.

"Well, whatever he uses, he takes the biggest swing in his life, and prays he doesn't have to hit him again. He checks for a pulse. There isn't one. 'Oh, my God,' he says. Maybe he's crying, mmm? Then he does the thing with the floppy whatsit, and whoops—there's the door. It's the wife. Kill her, too? No way. One killing a day's enough for this guy. He pulls on the mask, sneaks up behind her and pushes her into the pantry."

Stark sighed. He nodded, his mouth twisted resignedly, in acknowledgement that what Kowalski was saying had a ring of real logic.

Kowalski said: "So he goes home and he frets about the whole thing and he thinks, 'They're going to find something. They're going to suspect me.' He's desperate. 'Wait a minute, the wife. I'll pin it on the wife.' What's her name, Johnson, so he makes the note about the hidden entrance to the pantry. Bingo."

"Risky—the note, if he wrote it."

"Not really. Why would you think he wrote it? You don't know who it's from. Maybe you'll think it's—I don't know—some friend who thinks the wife is going to get away with it, or something. So he writes the note, leaves it at the desk downtown, and you're supposed to think the wife did it. You see what I mean. It has to be Bishop."

Stark looked for a long time at Kowalski, the wheels turning in his mind. Kowalski nodded, encouraging the thought process. Finally, Stark said, "Bishop."

"Bishop," Kowalski echoed with one final nod.

"Mmm—you want another beer?"

"I'm fine. You go ahead."

Stark gestured for the waitress. They sat in silence while she shuffled over. Stark clasped his hands over his stomach, tapping the thumbs together. The waitress cleared her throat. Stark looked up. "I'll have another."

"Okay," said Kowalski, "back with Bishop. So he bumps off Harper, does the thing with the note, and then you tell him about Chilly. So now he's really shaken up. The finger's pointing at him. You haven't arrested the wife, even though he's sent you the note. Maybe you didn't find the letter in the computer. And now you tell him that this Chilly can identify him and give him a motive for the murder.

"He's got no choice. You think he called Cataldi. Cataldi wouldn't help him. He'd just wash his hands of the whole thing. Believe me. Now, obviously he *did* call Cataldi and say he's gotten rid of the files that blew the cover off the stock scam. 'Course he didn't tell Cataldi that he'd killed Harper. Cataldi would put two and two together, but he wouldn't want to know.

"Then Cataldi talks to his computer whizbang and he says that's not good enough, that somebody like Payne, could find the files. And that *would* worry him. So that's when the dynamic duo go to the apartment and wipe out the whole freaking computer outfit—just to make sure. They don't know it's too late, that you've already seen the things. So Bishop is on his own. And now he's into it—not just over his head, but so far over his head he can't see the surface. He's broken his cherry. He's killed a guy. All bets are off. You tell him about Chilly and you scare the living shit out of him. Now, he's fighting for his life. He's not rational any more. He goes and finds Chilly, and like you said, he figures he'll make it look like a street crime, so he smashes the crap out of Chilly. He's frightened, he's terrified, he smashes and smashes and smashes and—there you go. I solved your case for you."

Chapter Sixteen

Bishop's reaction to being arrested wasn't what Stark had expected. There was no anguish, no tearful pleading, no final release of confession. There was fear, and he'd expected that. Bishop was tense, stuttering, disoriented, but he was also angry, indignant, outraged and finally almost resigned. Stark knew that he shouldn't be influenced by the reaction. Often, it was a giveaway.

But sometimes, with the smart ones, it wasn't. And Bishop was a smart one. Apart from protesting his innocence and threatening to sue for false arrest, he refused to say anything until he had seen his lawyer. In the event, his lawyer, a corporate and real estate guy, didn't come. Instead, he sent Ron Simms, a high flyer who spent most of his time in exotic foreign casinos or at a track. His fifty-five-inch girth and the chewed Cohiba cigars, so ever-present they seemed to be part of his face, were solid clues that it wasn't the kind of track you run around, but the kind where you watch horses or dogs do the running.

Simms supported his gambling habit by charging high-profile criminals—mostly mob types— a lot of money. They thought he was worth it because he almost always won—in one way or another, not necessarily getting them off completely, but having charges and sentences reduced to a level they could handle. He had a way of spinning cases out so long and being so irritating that Crown attorneys, watching their cost meter soar, would finally cave in. Just his showing up for the interview was going to cost Bishop a bundle. Most cops hated Simms' ample guts. Stark got a kick out of him.

They greeted each other with such amity that Bishop looked suspiciously from one to the other, as if he wondered whether he was going to be the *victim* of this friendly relationship. He needn't have worried. Stark gave them time in private, which amounted to five minutes before Simms shouted for him to come back into the room. Having settled on to a plastic-backed chair that buckled dangerously, Simms wasn't about to rise until it was time to leave. As soon as Stark entered, Simms pointed a stubby finger at him. He had a voice reminiscent of Sydney Greenstreet in the Maltese Falcon.

"You've charged us with murder in the first degree, two counts. Any questions we do choose to answer will pertain directly and only to those charges, you understand? We will answer nothing with respect to any other matters, Mr Bishop's financial dealings and business affairs, for example. Do you get my meaning? No illegal activity is being alleged with regard to those dealings, and no illegal activity took place in respect of those affairs, so we won't answer anything that has anything to do with that at all. Okay?"

Stark smiled wryly and shook his head. "They're all connected."

"First of all, we deny the murders. Since my client was involved with no crime, there can't be any connection to it. If you're bound to try to establish motive and then proceed from there to the crime you allege, you're wasting your time—and ours."

Stark started to say something, but Simms stopped him with a raised hand.

"Before you begin, there's one other thing. If you publish in any way any information that suggests illegal or unethical business behaviour by us, we will sue you and the police service and the civic government for one hell of a lot of money, and boy, we'll win. If there's any innuendo in the press, we'll subpoena the reporter and the editor and have them locked up until they give up the cop who tipped them. I mean it, Harry. This is a murder charge and that's it."

Stark stared at Simms and Bishop in turn, trying to decide which one looked more smug than the other. He chuckled. Of course Simms couldn't stop him from asking any questions he wanted to ask, but he decided to let the Delsim thing go for the moment. He'd have lots of time to push it later. He turned on the recorder, gave the time and location, his name and rank and had Bishop and the lawyer identify themselves. Then Stark looked at Bishop, and said: "Where were you on the night of Sunday, January 12, 1997?"

Simms had his hand on the back of Bishop's chair. Stark saw the hand move slightly and knew from past experience that it was the result of one finger's touching Bishop on the shoulder, which meant he could answer the question.

"The night Chris was killed, I was at home."

"All evening?"

"All day. I had the flu."

"Was anyone with you?"

"No."

"Where were you on the evening of Monday, January 20?"

"That was the day of Chris's funeral. Home again. They had a reception after the funeral, but I didn't go. I was feeling—too distraught, so I went straight home and I stayed there. And, no, there was no one with me. I was alone."

"Distraught? Why? Because of the emotion of the funeral, or because I told you about Chilly?"

"Chilly?" Simms said. "Who the hell's Chilly?"

"Horace MacIver, the man—one of the men—your client killed. He went by the name Chilly."

"The indigent?"

"Yeah."

The fat finger was pointing again. "Of all the aspects of this bizarre case, this is the most absurd. Do you really think a man in Mr Bishop's position in society and with his background and so on fraternizes with alley derelicts? How, in God's name, could he possibly have any connection with or even knowledge of the existence of this man?"

"Oh, he didn't know him. And I'm sure he'd never spoken to him before, although Chilly probably hit him up for a loonie or two."

"Hit him up for a loonie or two. What are you talking about?"

"He didn't know Chilly personally, but he knew who he was, and that was my mistake. You see, I didn't know Chilly lived in the alley. He didn't tell me. I thought he was just passing through. But Bishop knew who he was the moment I told him about the homeless guy who'd overheard an argument between two men behind The Purple."

"The what?" Simms had a strained expression of confusion, like someone asking directions to somewhere he wasn't sure he wanted to go.

"Ask him," Stark said, nodding to Bishop. "He knows the place well."

Simms turned with what looked like great effort and faced Bishop, who shrugged his shoulders and screwed his face in exaggerated puzzlement.

"My client has no idea what you're talking about."

"Oh, your client knows what I'm talking about, all right. He and his lover went there all the time."

"My what?"

"Your lover, Bishop. Your lover and your colleague—one and the same—Chris Harper."

Bishop's mouth fell open. His gaze jumped back and forth several times between Stark and Simms, who also had an expression of disbelief.

"The man is insane," Bishop said. Then, pointing at Stark: "You are out of your mind. You should be committed. I'm going to sue you for defamation of character, I promise you that. I'm going to sue him," he said to Simms, who quietened him with a waving hand, and said to Stark:

"Where on earth did you this wild and irresponsible and unconscionable allegation?"

"Who told you I was a bloody fairy. I'm no—queer. This is—grossly offensive. I want an apology."

"We would like an apology." Simms nodded.

"Well, you're not going to get one." Stark gathered up his papers and stood up. "This is going nowhere. You'll be arraigned tomorrow morning."

"Arraigned?" Bishop said. "Wait. This is absurd—"

"This is bloody awful police work, Stark. I'm not going to let you get away with this. You have no evidence on which to charge this man. This is just—"

"Save it. I'll see you tomorrow morning."

"Wait," said Bishop. "You're not going to keep me here? I can go home—"

Simms patted him on the shoulder. "I'm afraid you won't be able to go home, Shane—until tomorrow." He looked meaningfully at Stark. "It's only for tonight. Tomorrow, when we go before a judge, I'll get you out. I'll get this case thrown out. Don't you worry."

****

Judge Walter Franks hated Saturday morning duty. He hated the punk prosecutors for their ignorance and stupidity. He hated the defence lawyers for being too well-dressed or wearing too much jewelry or being sycophantic or being indignant. He hated the self-righteous and the sleazy, the swine and the scum. He loved curling. It was the only thing he liked about winter, and he wasn't curling.

"Next, what's next?"

The clerk read the information against Bishop in a rapid and almost inaudible monotone. Stark watched Bishop. He was shaking in the dock. His night in the detention centre must have really rattled him—as Stark had hoped.

"Date?"

"February twenty two," said the young Crown, Douglas Marsters. Simms consulted his diary.

"That's fine," he said.

"Next," the judge said.

"Uh, your honour—"

The judge sighed. "What is it, Mr Simms?"

"I'd like to speak to bail."

"Bail?" Franks looked at Simms with a mixture of shock and revulsion, as if he'd just seen something

163

moving in his salad. "On a charge of premeditated double murder?"

"Two separate counts, your honour, and they're—"

"All right, two counts, so what? Bail? Don't be ridiculous. What are you talking about? Don't try to pull your stunts in here."

"The law allows, in unusual circumstances—"

"Don't tell me the law, Mr Simms What unusual circumstances? Your client suddenly turn into an eighty-year-old, blind, crippled nun with acute angina? You're wasting my time—we've got reams of work to do—now, clear out, I'm warning you."

"Your honour—"

"What now?"

"I want to make a motion to quash these charges as completely unsubstantiated, with no grounds for proceeding—in fact a malicious prosecution."

"Mr Simms, listen to me. You're not making any motions here. You want to make a motion, go to a belly-dancing class. Otherwise, wait till Monday and find yourself another judge. I'm sure you will. Now let's get on with this. Next."

As the policeman led him away, Bishop looked imploringly at Simms, who responded by making downward motions with both hands, as if he was trying to calm a frightened child. When Bishop was gone, Simms turned and gave Stark a look of disgust.

Before the start of court, Marsters, the Crown, had told Stark, in a high-pitched, kid's voice, that the Crown Attorney was not comfortable with these charges, and that he had been instructed to tell Stark that it was only out of respect for his ability and experience that they were proceeding with the case at all, and that the Crown was giving Stark three days to produce some hard evidence that linked Bishop with these killings or he would withdraw the charges and would have something to say to Stark's superiors.

"Frankly, Detective—" the kid squeaked "—all you have, according to your report, is evidence of a possible motive, not a scrap of evidence to put Bishop at the scene of either crime, and the alleged murderer—"

"The man alleged to be a murderer."

"I'm sorry, what—?"

"Just correcting your grammar. Never mind."

"The alleged murderer is a respected businessman, with no record of violence—there's nothing in his background to suggest he's capable of anything like this—"

"Anyone's capable of anything—if they're pushed hard enough. He did it all right. By Monday, he'll be a quivering mass of jelly, begging to confess."

"Don't you think that might be wishful thinking?"

"What the fuck do you know, kid?"

****

"You know that stock you were interested in, Delsim?" The message light on Stark's phone had been flashing when he got back from court. The message had been left the night before, but after a heavy evening at Carbo's, Stark had flopped, fully dressed, on to the crumpled bedclothes and had taken immediate refuge in oblivion. Now he was returning the call to Charlie Hayden.

"What about it?"

"It's taken off—like a bloody skyrocket, and no wonder."

"No wonder?"

"Bream released the BH report on Royal Cross."

"What? That doesn't make any sense."

"What do you mean?"

"I mean. I've got the report—"

"You do? See here, old boy, that's not quite playing the game. Why didn't you let me have it? I mean, co-operation is a two-way street, old chap—"

"I couldn't, Charlie. I'm sorry. It's evidence in a murder case. But it doesn't make any sense."

"So you said."

"I took the report to a professor, the guy you told me about at U of T. He said, without any hesitation or doubt, that the report showed the Royal Cross site was useless. There was nothing there."

"Well, that's not what the report Bream released shows. It's a bloody motherlode. You're sure he wasn't holding it upside down, or something? Look, now that the report is out, do you mind sending me a copy of what you have? It's possible somebody's made a mistake. I promise you that I won't do anything with it until you give me the go-ahead, but I'd like to have somebody look at it, if you don't mind."

"I'll send it right over, Charlie. Let me know what you find."

****

Stark was in the Identification Unit evidence locker on the sixth floor of headquarters. He was looking through the box of material that had been removed from the Harper/Johnson apartment. He was holding a hiking boot in one hand and flipping through large photographic prints with the other. He found what he was looking for, a picture of the footprint in the snow.

The boot he had in his hand was one he'd found in

Bishop's apartment, after getting a warrant to search the place. When he'd found the boots in Bishop's closet, he thought he recognized them as identical to the pair he'd found in the cupboard in the garage. He could have compared boot with boot, but the wife was now back living in the apartment, after he had given his clearance.

He turned the boot over and compared the print with the photograph. They were identical. The size of the photographic print had been adjusted to match measurements taken at the scene, so the picture was the actual size of the print. He placed the boot on it and it fit perfectly. Size 9. Not unusual—one of the most common foot sizes, and it struck him that it wouldn't be unusual, either, for Bishop and Harper to buy the same boots, and probably at the same store. They were rugged boots, expensive, insulated, waterproof—perfect for exploring jagged rock faces and sodden jungles. Harper would have bought his for function. Bishop's might have been for form. He was, after all, supposed to be a geologist.

Stark riffled through the evidence box. There wasn't much there—a few odds and ends the ident officers had thought might be significant, anything that had seemed to them to have been out of place. They meant nothing to Stark.

Mostly, it contained the photographs they'd found scattered on the floor. He glanced at them all, studied some a little longer. Most of them were pictures of Harper in various wildernesses—from barren tundra to leafy jungle, standing in front of tents like a 19th century explorer, holding chunks of rock and grinning with the same boyish expression he'd displayed on the magazine cover.

There were a few of Harper and Johnson in hiking

gear beside rushing rivers and gazing over mountainous vistas, and several of the couple on what must have been a cycling holiday in England, posed with their backpacks and bikes in front of country pubs and ruined abbeys.

There were some skiing pictures, with Bishop included in some and one of Harper and Johnson and Christine Harvey standing in front of a ski lodge. He put the photos on the table and continued rummaging through the box. And then he found something he hadn't seen before: sealed in a polyethylene bag, a piece of paper, a ticket, a lift-ticket from the Blue Peaks ski lodge, a ticket stamped Sunday, January 12.

Angrily, Stark jerked his cell phone out of his jacket pocket, whipped up the antenna and punched in the number of 55 Division. He got Cory on the line.

"What do you know about this lift ticket?"

"The what?"

"A ski-lift ticket from Blue Peaks—in the evidence box. The Harper case—remember?"

"Hey, give me a break. The Harper case is yours, not mine. I mean, I was just at the scene. That's the limit of my involvement."

"Where was the lift ticket found? And why wasn't I told about it?"

"I think they found it—"

"You think? Don't think. Know."

"They found it in the back yard. And you were told about it. It was in my report."

"In your report? I don't care about the god-damned report. Why didn't you tell me about it on the night?"

"I didn't think it was—I mean, it was a break-in. I figured the ski ticket was one of theirs. They're both yuppies—skiers, you know what I mean—"

"Jesus Christ."

Chapter Seventeen

Stark picked up a mug shot of Bishop and headed north on Highway 400.

It had snowed heavily the night before, and coming after a long dry spell, the snowfall had infected a lot of avid skiers with the twenty-four-hour flu, which they were curing with a day on the slopes. Despite the blowing snow drifting across the highway, a steady stream of them in their mandatory four-wheel drives, bristling with skis, flowed rapidly past Stark, who clung to the inside lane, gripped the wheel tightly and never exceeded eighty kilometres an hour for one hundred and fifty kilometres in a car that was fitted with all-season tires in an area that called for proper snow tires.

The worst was yet to come, as he turned gingerly off the highway and on to a county road, the surface of which was snow-covered but for two pairs of tracks etched by previous vehicles, tracks punctuated by patches of ice.

Stark slowed to a crawl, causing a line of traffic to form behind him, with drivers impatiently craning to see what variety of cretin was holding them up, delaying their alpine delights. Things deteriorated rapidly when Stark had to turn off the county road on to the side road that led to Blue Peaks itself.

That road was covered with a thick layer of icy snow. The vehicle tracks were hard-packed grooves you had to stick to or risk sliding off into a deep ditch. Stark's Chev wasn't built for roads like this. The four-wheel drives behind him were, but even they couldn't risk passing in these conditions on the narrow road. So he led a procession into the Blue Peaks parking lot, a procession that roared past him, each driver in turn glaring at the huddled figure in the oversized parka who was parking his car at the first available spot.

As Stark trudged past them on his way to the lodge, the angry drivers were still glaring at him while they unloaded their skis and boots, particularly since it was apparent that the person who had held them up wasn't there to ski. Stark made a face at them.

He spent the first half hour over two double Scotches in the lounge. When the shaking had subsided sufficiently, he called the bartender over, flashed his badge at him and asked him whether he knew the fellow whose picture he was showing him.

The bartender shook his head. "Who is he? Am I supposed to know him?"

"He skis here."

The bartender gave a half laugh and cast around with his arm at the crowded bar. "So does half the world. There's a few regulars I know, of course, but he's not one of 'em. Sorry."

Stark was irrationally disappointed with the response. The idea that he might be able to find someone who would recognize Bishop was absurd. Finally, he had to concede that he was being ridiculous. He caught the bartender's eye again.

"Yes, sir, another?"

"No, that's fine. What do I owe you?"

"Fourteen-fifty."

"Let me ask you this. Supposing somebody was a regular here, who would be the most likely person in the place to know him?"

"Karin Shula. She's the program director, events co-ordinator. If anybody knew, she probably would." Stark asked him where he could find this woman, which led him to an office on the second floor.

Stark expected to find a virago in ski gear. Instead, his hand was shaken by a woman who came around from behind a desk in a pin-striped, charcoal suit, with a skirt that was longer than he would have liked. Her hair was almost white, blonde only in comparison with the brilliant white of the snow through the window behind her. Her eyes were as blue as an August sky. It flashed through his mind that it was too bad he wasn't looking for someone who remembered seeing *her* instead of Bishop. Those eyes were unforgettable.

"How can I help you, Detective. You're a long way off your beat, aren't you?" She smiled, revealing a row of gleaming, perfect teeth

He showed her the picture. Her response was as negative as the bartender's.

"Sorry," she said. "We get—"

"Yeah, I know, thousands of people. Is there anyone else who might recognize somebody?"

"The ski pro. Scott. If the man took skiing lessons. He might."

Stark got directions to find Scott, at the pro shop. He turned out to be exactly as Stark had imagined he would be, a caricature of a ski instructor: tall, with a tousled mane of sandy curls, a caramel tan, with reindeer running across the front of a roll-necked sweater that wasn't bulky enough to conceal the wide shoulders and thick arms. He shook Stark's hand with a crushing grip.

"That coat's no good for skiing, Inspector—"

"Just Detective. And I'm not here to ski."

"You're not? Well, what then?"

Almost reluctantly, fearing disappointment, Stark showed him the picture.

"Holy shit, the guy who killed Harper."

Stark's head jerked back in surprise.

"What? How d'you know that?"

"It was in the paper."

"But how did you recognize him so quickly?

"Because I know him."

"You know him? Personally?"

"No, no. He used to ski here. I gave him lessons. Actually, I remember the Harper couple better, her especially. Cute little thing and I never thought, you know, that she and the hubby—I mean, I don't think he could have—you know—he was a bit of a wimp. Maybe that's not nice to say about a dead guy—but anyway."

"What about the guy in the picture? Do you know his name? I mean, do you know him of your own knowledge and not from what you read in the paper?"

"Oh yeah, I knew him. Lousy skier, lousy athlete, big but—soft, you know. Pear-shaped, not fat, you know, but shoulders sloped, too narrow, ass was too big. He tried—he got to know a few basics, you know, but he'd never make a good skier. Now the chick, she was great. She is great. She and hubby, they ski here a lot. More her than him. The three of them came together, the Bishop guy and the couple. Kind of ironic, eh? Him killin' him and all?"

"You said Bishop *used* to come here?"

"That's right. I haven't seen him—in a while. I don't

think I've seen him this year. 'Course he could still be coming here. He could ski here every day for that matter, and I might never see him. It's just that, when he was skiing fairly regularly—two or three years ago, and then even after that, every time he came, he'd drop in to see me because he always had some problem or other from the last time, and he'd ask me about it and I'd give him a tip—and he'd give *me* a tip. Very generous guy. That's how I remember him so well. So if he's still skiing, he's either gotten stingy or he thinks he knows enough."

"So there's no way you'd know, or anybody here would know, whether he came here on Sunday, January 12?"

Scott shook his head. "Not unless he stayed over. Then they'd have him in the lodge register. But I haven't seen him this year. I can tell you that for sure."

Stark checked at the lodge, but Bishop had not been registered on the weekend of the twelfth. At least he knew Bishop skied, that he had skied there in the past, and that he could have been there on the twelfth, and the lift ticket could have been his. It could also have been Chris Harper's or Dianne Johnson's, of course, except that Johnson was away with the car that day and if someone else had taken Harper skiing, Stark would have run across him by now—unless, of course, Harper had gone skiing with Bishop. But surely there'd have been some sign that he'd been skiing that day, and would he have wanted to go skiing after a night of partying? He knew the wife didn't ski that day. Carol Weems had called the number Johnson had given her of the school friend in Ottawa, and the woman had told her that Dianne had spent the weekend with her, leaving some time mid-morning. With snowy roads and a couple of stops along

174

the way, that would have got her home right when she said she got there, and certainly wouldn't have given her time to stop for a ski along the way.

There was a message on Stark's cell phone when he got back to the car. Actually, he'd heard it ring on his way up the 400, but there was no way he was going to take his hands off the wheel then to answer it. The message was from Charlie Hayden.

"Stark, old boy, you've got it wrong. You've got the wrong survey report. There's a second report that corrects the first one—poor drill samples, or something, according to Bream. I'm no expert. Anyway, the second report says they've hit paydirt, a mountain full of glittery yellow stuff. The shares are still going up, old boy. There are even rumours of a takeover bid. Talk to you later."

****

Stark decided to confront Bishop with the lift ticket. He might even try stretching the truth by saying that the ski pro spotted him on the slopes on the Sunday. Then, the hell with what Simms had said, he would pump Bishop about X-King and his relationship with Harper, pump him till it all came out. He figured that a few nights with the lads in the Don Jail would have shaken something loose. He was right.

Of course he had to call Simms in for the interview. The big man had no clients or court that day, so he was dressed casually, in an enormous knit sweater in a pattern of maroon and grey whorls. He reminded Stark of a hot-air balloon. He had an unlit Churchillian cigar clenched in his teeth, and the guard snapped at him that there was no smoking.

"Don't worry, Caliban, I'm not going to light the thing."

"Good thing he doesn't know Shakespeare," Stark said quietly.

"Huh, no chance of that, but I see you do. I'm not surprised. What's this all about, Stark? I was working on a motion to get him out of here this afternoon. You get the invitation?"

"Nope."

"Well, the Crown has it. Curiously enough, I was going to call you before you called me. My client has something to say that I think will end this nonsense without a hearing, in any event."

"Glad to hear it."

"Oh, I don't think you will be. You really screwed up this time, Stark. I'm sure he'll want to sue you for false arrest. Anyway, don't worry about it, because I know we wouldn't win—but we will want a written apology and a full statement to the press that completely exonerates him."

"You'll be lucky."

"Yes, I think you'll find I might well be. Ah, here he is."

Bishop shuffled into the interview room, head down, face drooping. If Stark had ever seen a beaten man, he was looking at him now.

"God, you look awful," Simms said with affected concern. "What have you been doing to this man?"

Stark shook his head and smiled sardonically. Simms' pomposity was part of the act for the client's benefit. He had once explained to Stark, "Justice must be seen to be done, or the client thinks he's paying for nothing—which often he is."

"I have something to show you, Mr Bishop," Stark said.

"No, no," Bishop said, shaking his head.

"'No, no?' What do you mean, 'no, no?' I have something to show you." Stark began to take the lift ticket out of his pocket, but Bishop said:

"Before you show me anything, I have something to tell you."

Stark shrugged. "Go ahead."

"I have—an alibi."

"Oh yes? For both killings, I suppose."

"As a matter of fact—yes."

"Wait a minute, now. Let me guess. You were suffering from amnesia. You hit your head on your bunk and it all came back to you?"

Simms started a blustering protest. Bishop silenced him with the tired raising of an arm. He looked at Stark with defeated eyes.

"Look, Stark," he said, "you don't know what you've done to me. You've ruined me. When this is over you're going to apologize. And not because I'm going to demand it, but because I think you're a decent man, and you're going to feel terrible. Because you've made a very bad mistake, you've bungled this altogether. And now, having humiliated me to this extent, you're going to force me to further embarrass myself by leaving me no choice but to reveal an aspect of my personal life that I have disclosed to not a living soul before this."

He gave Stark a grim look as if to suggest that some sort of sombre event was about to take place and Stark should be aware of the anguish he was instigating.

Stark returned a look of indifference. "I'm waiting," he said after a long moment's silence.

Bishop sighed, then said, "If you give me a pen and paper—" Simms snapped open his briefcase with remarkable speed. Stark pictured the item on the bill: "Stationery and writing utensil—twenty five dollars."

Bishop unscrewed the top of the proffered Mont Blanc ("Maybe $40," Stark thought), wrote something on a yellow, legal-sized pad and pushed it across the table to Stark.

"That," he said, "is the name of a woman I visit from time to time. She will tell you that I was with her on the days in question. On the Sunday that Chris was killed, I was there from one in the afternoon to well past midnight. On the day of the funeral, when this other fellow was killed, I went there right after the funeral and stayed all night."

****

The address was an apartment near Bathurst and St. Clair, an old red brick building with stone cornices and lintels, and leaded windows. Apartment 514 was on the top floor, reached by a creaking elevator not much bigger than a phone booth. Apart from the ancient elevator, which worked smoothly enough despite being slow and noisy, the building was perfectly restored, with new hall carpets that split rows of black-and-white tiles, the halls lit by strips of concealed fluorescent tubes along each side of the ceiling, the walls punctuated by candle-flame light bulbs supported by yellow tubes.

Apartment 514 was at the end of the hall. Stark studied the door. There was something odd about it. He pressed the buzzer and waited. Seconds passed, and he was about to try knocking when he heard a noise. Someone was behind the door. Locks clicked and the door swung slowly open.

He was looking at eye level. As the gap from the door to the jamb widened, no figure came into view.

Then his peripheral vision caught a shape below eye level. His head snapped down. For a split second he thought he was looking at a child, but only for a split second. For this child was wearing a black negligée, with a low bodice that revealed much of two well-rounded, apple-sized breasts.

This was a miniature woman, and apart from a face that was just slightly elfish, a perfectly proportioned reduction. He had to stifle a laugh—not at the little woman's appearance, because she was quite beautiful, despite the hooker make-up—but because of the revelation that Bishop liked to get it on with a midget. "A 'little person,' he politically corrected his thought, which made the laugh even harder to suppress, and it finally escaped in a burbled spurt when the woman said, with a lascivious grin, "What can I do for you, *big* boy?"

When Stark laughed, the woman's grin vanished, to be replaced by a scowl, and she said indignantly, "Something funny?"

Stark put a hand up in protest. "No, no. It's not— I'm sorry, it's just I wasn't expecting—listen—" Awkwardly, he fished in a pocket for his badge, showed it to her.

"Detective? Well. The *chief* give you my address, did he?"

Stark smiled. "No, not the chief. Do you think we might go inside?"

She shrugged and stood aside, gesturing extravagantly for him to enter, and he walked into a small, tastefully decorated living room.

A trash-TV host moralized about something or other on a large-screen set in one corner. A half-eaten bowl of Cheerios sat on an end table beside a big leather recliner he thought the little woman must get lost in.

"I wasn't expecting company," she said. Her voice was husky, somewhere between a child's and an adult's in tone and pitch. She walked past him with an exaggerated stride, swaying her tiny hips like a small-scale Mae West and clambered on to the big chair, revealing a curve of thigh shapely enough to make Stark breathe in sharply.

But no sooner had the thought entered his mind than he shooed it away. Despite her attractiveness, he thought he would feel a little too kinky doing it with a "little person." It would be like having it off with a child, he thought. He couldn't understand the appeal she had for Bishop, and he wasn't about to try.

"Isn't this ridiculous?" she said.

"What's that?"

"This guy on the TV. He's got people who married or shacked up with their ex-wives' relatives. One guy ran off with his ex's sister; one woman married her ex-husband's son, for Christ's sake. It's disgusting. And then he's got the ex-wives and husbands on there, too. 'Course they're all yelling and screaming and about to hit each other. These shows are always the same. Daytime TV, eh? What can you do?

"So, Detective, to what do I owe this little visit. I know you're not Morality. You look like too nice a guy. Besides, by now, you'd have your pants down and your dick out and telling me to hurry up because you're double-parked." She smiled affectedly, then laughed when she saw that two of the participants on the TV show were standing nose to nose and shouting at each other like a baseball manager and an umpire. "Look at that," she said. "Look at that. Fucking ridiculous, eh?"

"Do you have a client called Shane Bishop?"

"Oh, I don't give out my client's names, Detective. That wouldn't be professional. It'd be unethical."

"Let me explain." Stark showed the Bishop's mug shot. This gentleman says he's a client of yours. Now he's facing two counts of first-degree murder—"

"Holy cow."

"—and he says that when these killings took place, he was here with you."

"Mmm."

"Now, he seems to think that you'll tell me that he was here. Otherwise, he wouldn't have sent me, would he? And I'm not from the Morality Squad. I'm Homicide. I'm not asking you to betray a confidence. It's obvious I wouldn't know you existed unless he had told me. Doesn't that make sense?"

"Mmm. I guess so. All right, I know Shane—the gunslinger."

Stark chuckled. "I don't think I want to know why you call him that."

She giggled. "Nothing weird. It's because his name is Shane, you know, like Alan Ladd in the old cowboy movie. Remember, he didn't want to do anymore gunfighting—"

"I remember. What about—*this* Shane?"

She scuttled across to the other side of the chair, and bent over the arm, revealing even more thigh this time, and she came up with a big agenda book.

"Okay, what dates?"

"Two things. First I want *you* to tell me the dates he was here, and second I want to see the entries in that book."

"Oh no. Oh no." Her voice had an adamant quaver.

"There're names in here that could blow the lid off the city—lawyers, doctors, city councillors. I even have a regular visit from the mayor of one of those suburban cities. No, no. I can't let you see this."

"Here's what you do. Get a couple of sheets of paper. Cover up all the other names, and just show me the entries for Bishop, okay?"

She pondered that for a moment and finally shrugged. "Yeah, I guess that would be all right. But I hold the book." She pointed a finger at him.

"Sure."

"Okay, let me see—" She gave Stark five recent dates. Two of them were of the days of the killings. Then she ripped out sheets of paper from the back of the agenda and used them to conceal the other names, while she showed Stark all the entries for Bishop. They were all listed as "Gunslinger." They showed the time of the appointment. She showed Stark the date at the top of the page, but there was no indication of how long he had spent on each occasion.

"All right, your book says he was here. How do I know he wasn't here for five minutes each time?"

"See this, the number 7? That means he was here seven hours on that date. I charge by the hour. Then this one, it has AN beside it. That means an all-nighter. I got a special rate for that. Would you like to know my rates, Detective?" She smiled archly.

"Thanks, anyway—"

"Look at that. They're actually wrestling with each other. Here come the security guys. Can you believe it? There are sure a lot of weird people in the world, eh—"

When the little woman closed the door behind him, telling him, without irony, to call any time and she'd give him a reduced rate, Stark looked at the door again. Then he realized what was odd about it. The peephole was at the level of his navel.

Chapter Eighteen

It wasn't because of the agenda entries of the little hooker, who'd given her name as Carla Mowat, that Stark had to let Bishop loose. The alibis were much too convenient. He had little difficulty imagining that Bishop paid the woman to put his name in the book on the pertinent dates. He thought about threatening her, but figured it would be a waste of time.

He could always pull her in later if he had to. Anyway, it was more effective to let people think they've got away with something and then come back at them. He was convinced that Bishop was the killer—but it was still mainly gut feeling and strong motive that were doing the convincing. Everything about Bishop was contrived. He was a complete phony, and not the least because he'd hired Ron Simms, who, to Stark's knowledge, had never represented anybody who wasn't guilty.

In the end, Stark had to let Bishop go because of two phone calls. Actually, he didn't want let Bishop go. Marsters, the Crown, dropped the charges. The first phone call was from John Tilman, the cop who'd told him about Chilly's killing. Again, Stark didn't remember his name. Tilman again reminded him that they'd worked together on the Cassidy case—whatever that was.

"We tried to call you this morning, it being your case and all, but I guess your cell phone was switched off or something and the dispatcher couldn't reach you on the radio—"

"What case are you talking about—John?"

"MacIver, the homeless guy."

"What about him?"

"We got the guys who did it. My partner and I."

"What?"

"We were patrolling in the same area last night, different alley, and we came across these two punks—ah, you wouldn't believe 'em. Rings through their noses and their fucking nipples. Heads shaved, Doc Marten's, Nazi tattoos, real skinheads. And one of them was wearing—get this—a long leather coat just like the one the other wino, Boozehead, or whatever his name was, told us that Chilly had got.

"We come across these two beating up on some— *homeless person*, beatin' the shit out of the guy with a baseball bat. Smashed one leg all to shit, broke his ribs. They tried to scram, but we grabbed 'em. Actually, I gotta admit, it was my partner nabbed 'em—she's a girl, you know, but strong, and fast and tough as a—I think she's a—anyway, she collared 'em. So we took 'em in to the station and they right away started to sing, like they were proud of it, and they didn't want to miss the chance to go down for it. They told us they killed the other wino, Chilly. Said they had a mission—a mission, can you imagine, a fucking mission. Said they were out to rid the city of undesirables. I told 'em I couldn't think of anything more undesirable than them. And, guess what?"

"What?"

"Polaroids."

"What?"

"The fucking scum had Polaroid pictures of the poor

wino. They took pictures of Chilly with his face all smashed. One of them's holding Chilly up and smiling at the camera. Can you imagine? Unbelievable. Anyway, we got 'em here if you want to interview 'em. It's still your case—but I guess, you know, the collar's ours, eh?"

"What? Oh yeah, right, sure. Great. Thanks," Stark said, distracted, stunned.

The second call was from Marsters.

"I dropped the charges against Bishop an hour ago. I guess you know why, or do you?"

"I know."

"I don't know why you thought you had a case against him in the first place. I really think—"

Stark hung up on him. "Prick."

****

Sid Holtzman was spreading cream cheese on a bagel for a sour-faced, bony woman in a leather jacket who was sitting at the counter and watching every move Sid made.

"Hey, Harry, haven't seen you in a while. Grab a pew. I'll be with you in a minute." The woman turned and glowered at Stark, as if he might be responsible for her not getting enough attention paid to her bagel.

"So, how's the case going?" Sid said as he slid into the booth opposite Harry.

"Don't ask."

"That bad, eh? I see the wife's moved back home."

"You know her?"

"Not really, but Roberta, you know, Berkowski—she's such a nosy bitch, knows everybody's business—she was in here yesterday. The woman walked by with another chick. Roberta pointed her out. Real chummy they were, arm in arm."

"Oh, yeah. Probably her sister. Was she tall, the other woman?"

"I don't know. I didn't pay no attention. Just a woman is all. Plain, I think. Maybe not. You know me and women. Now horses, whoo-hoo—fillies. I like fillies, Stark. You think I'm weird?"

"I think you're smart."

"Want a coffee? I shoulda brought one over. I'll get you one." He brought back two steaming mugs, and removed the paper ring from a cigar. "That's the right way to do it, you know, Harry. My cousin David told me."

"How's that?"

"The ring, the paper ring on a cigar?"

"What about it?"

"You always should take it off before you smoke it. Otherwise, he says, it's *vulgar,* like showin' off, you know, that you've got an expensive cigar. Course he says my diamond ring is vulgar, too. 'Not right for a man to wear a diamond,' he says, 'too ostentatious,' he says. I say if you've got it, flaunt it. Course there's not much point with cigars. Nobody knows what David calls the 'correct etiquette' anyway, and they don't know one friggin' cigar from another. So they don't know what you paid for it, anyway. So, on the one hand I could be 'incorrect' and show off, but nobody would know I *had* something to show off in the first place, and they wouldn't even know that I *was* showing off. On the other hand, I could be 'correct,' and nobody would know I was being that, either. So, I guess it don't make no difference, right?"

"Jesus," Stark said, shaking his head

The woman at the counter spoke. She had a voice

with needles in it. "You're not going to smoke that thing, are you?"

Sid gave her a bland look, looked back at the cigar. "What, this?" he said. "This is not a thing, lady. This is a good cigar, not the cheap crap—excuse me—that I usually smoke. My cousin brought this back from Cuba for me."

"If you light that, I'm leaving, and I'm never coming back, and neither, I can assure you, will any of my friends."

"That's up to you, lady. You paid already. You can eat the rest of your bagel in here where it's nice and warm, or you can eat it out on the street and freeze your tush off. It's entirely up to you." Holtzman struck a match, let the sulphur burn off, then held the flame under the end of the cigar, rolling it with practised dexterity. The woman spun off the stool and strode out of the shop.

"Good riddance to bad rubbish," Sid said. "What a schnook."

Stark chuckled. "How many customers do you think your cigars cost you, Sid? Not to mention my Gauloises."

"Never mind your Gauloises. The day you can't smoke your cigarettes in Sid Holtzman's establishment's the day the place'll be closed down. You know what I get for customers? I get all the smokers who can't light up in the rest of the joints. I do all right. Why would I want more? I got good investments. My cousin David's a broker, you know. He's got me in all the right things. Besides, if I start making more money, my ex-wife'll be on me like a lamprey eel."

"What are you going to do when they ban smoking altogether in restaurants? They're going to do that eventually, you know. This is 1997, Sid, almost the end of the millennium. In the new millennium, I figure they'll make smokers wear a big 'S' on their chests, and force them to smoke outside in a cage."

Sid gave a dismissive wave and leaned forward conspiratorially. "I got it figured. Right where this little three-table smoking section is I'll put up a wall, with a door marked 'private.' That way it's not part of the restaurant, right? And you and I and some of the regulars will be allowed in there, and we can smoke to our hearts' content. What do you think?"

"Why not, Sid? Whatever you say." Stark shook his head.

"Now, let me see, there's a horse that's running at Gulfstream—"

****

When he got back to his apartment, Stark found a message on his phone from somebody called Philip Symchuk, who said he was answering a message Stark had left on his voice mail. He left a home number. Stark racked his brain. The name was familiar, but he couldn't place it. Finally, he recalled that Symchuk was the missing guy from the list of Harper's soirée guests. He called the number.

Symchuk, it seemed, had just arrived home from Africa, where he'd been out of touch for two weeks, "tramping through thick jungle."

"Looking for black stuff—thick, runny black stuff you drill holes in the ground for. Anyway, how can I help you—Detective, isn't it? Have my parking tickets caught up with me?"

"It's about Chris Harper, Mr Symchuk."

"Chris? Why, what's he done? Chris wouldn't do

anything illegal to save his life."

"You haven't talked to anyone since your return?"

"Not a soul. Got a message from my ex-wife to call her. But I'm not going to. What about Chris?"

"I'm afraid he's dead, Mr Symchuk."

"What do you mean, dead?"

"Just—"

"Dead? He can't be dead. He's—he's a young man, absolutely fit. Dead. My God. Was it an accident? A car crash? That damn little car of his. I told him a hundred times to get a Land Rover. He could afford it, for God's sake."

"It wasn't an accident, Mr Symchuk. I'm sorry to say, he was murdered."

"Murdered? What? That's impossible. I don't believe it. That's—Oh my God. Uh—look, I can't—I can't talk like this. Can you come round? I'll give you the address—murdered, my God—"

Symchuk's condo was beside Harbourfront, an open-plan clamour of chrome and glass and marble with a two-storey ceiling and a mezzanine bedroom reached by a tightly spiralled staircase. It was all white and gold and silver—long, white drapes bordering a twenty-foot-high window overlooking the twinkling lights of the harbour.

Symchuk was an ordinary-looking man, physically average in every way—about five-nine, neatly trimmed mousy-coloured hair, medium build, no facial hair, about thirty-five, neither handsome nor ugly—the perfect bank robber. But his clothing was far from ordinary. An outfit right out of a thirties movie—a navy-and-gold embroidered smoking jacket, a burnished-gold cravat, navy silk pyjama trousers and ox-blood slippers. It needed only a martini glass to complete the effect. But a single-malt (Stark didn't recognize the brand) in a Waterford old-fashioned glass was close.

Symchuk splashed about a three-finger measure in a matching glass for Stark. It ran down Stark's throat like liquid honey. They sat on facing egg-shell-coloured, curving leather couches that encircled an immense coffee table—a round, inch-thick slab of clear glass supported by an irregular chunk of granite.

Symchuk took a gulp of Scotch and a deep breath. "Tell me about Chris. What happened?"

"He was attacked in his apartment—by a person unknown—struck on the back of the head with a heavy object—also unidentified. He died almost instantly."

"So he wouldn't have felt anything—"

"No. He didn't even know it was coming."

"But who would do such a thing? Have you arrested somebody?"

Stark shifted uncomfortably. "We did arrest his partner, Shane Bishop."

Symchuk gasped.

"That's ridiculous. Why—it's absurd. He couldn't do such a thing—and for God's sake, why would he? I've never heard anything so absurd."

"Well, we had reason to believe—all right, I can't get into that. Anyway, the charges have been dropped."

"Thank God for that, but what possible reason could he have? Why would you ever think Shane could have killed anybody, let alone Chris?"

"For the moment, let's just leave it that the charges have been dropped."

"You may want to leave it at that, but if you won't tell me, I'll have to make some inquiries of my own."

"Whatever you like. Look, the reason I called you was that you were among a group of people who attended a party at Harper's the night before he was killed."

"When was he killed, exactly?"

"Early Sunday night, January twelfth."

"Yes, we had dinner and a few drinks at Chris's on Saturday, the eleventh, that's right. I left the next day. What did you want to know?"

Stark took another sip of the Scotch. There wasn't really much he did want to know that he didn't think he knew already. If Symchuk hadn't asked him to come to his home, he probably wouldn't have bothered to ask him anything. "I'm not sure you can help me, Mr Symchuk. It's rather a long way on in the investigation—"

"All right. Listen, before you go—this is bothering me. I'd like to know—if you can't tell me why you suspected Shane—at least tell me about the killing. Obviously, you don't think it was a robbery or something like that, or you wouldn't have thought it was Shane."

"Early indications were that it was a break-in—but I think that's unlikely. I believe that whoever killed Harper knew him. That Harper knew the person was in the apartment, and that he had no reason to suspect he was about to be attacked."

"Oh my God." He shook his head. "But what could be the motive? I mean, everyone liked Chris. He didn't have enemies or anything. He—he was a wonderful person, a brilliant geologist."

"Well, that's sort of the thing I want to know from you. Kind of standard questions really, and you've probably answered all of them."

"Could it have been a woman who killed him?"

"Why do you ask that?"

"Could it?"

"It's possible."

Symchuk looked at the Scotch in his glass as if it might tell him whether he should say what he was about to say. Without looking up, he asked: "Have you thought about the possibility that his wife might have done it?" Having broached the subject, he lifted his gaze to look at Stark, without moving his head. Then, apparently satisfied that Stark wasn't making any dismissive gestures, he raised one eyebrow and settled back on the sofa to await the answer. Stark looked hard at him for a moment, then averted his gaze as he took another sip of his drink. He sloshed the amber liquid in the bottom of the oversized glass, and finally said, "You tell me. Do *you* think that's a possibility?"

"Well, if you'd asked me before it happened whether I thought Dianne was capable of killing her husband, I'd have said, 'No way. Impossible.' But since you say it must have been somebody Chris knew—if you asked me if anyone he knew was—if anyone could have reason to kill him. And I mean you have to emphasize *anyone,* because the idea is still bizarre. But if *anyon*e Chris knew might have reason to kill him, it would be Dianne."

"Why do you say that? I've been told they were the perfect couple. Synergistic, I think somebody called it. They loved each other and so on."

"Well, there was some trouble in paradise."

"Tell me more."

"Listen, maybe I shouldn't be telling you anything, because—I mean, as I say, it's completely bizarre. But if it had to be—"

"Yes, I know, *anyone. "*

193

"Yes, if it had to be someone he knew, then the only person I can think of is her."

"Why?"

"Why, is that they were no longer the perfect couple. Chris hadn't changed. He was still the perfect husband—but she. Do you know anything about her?"

"As a matter of fact, I do."

"Do you know that she kept shooting herself in the foot—professionally?"

"Somebody did tell me something like that, yes."

Symchuk adjusted his cravat and tucked in the lapel of his jacket. He rested one elbow on the arm of the couch, the hand opened, palm up.

"They were great competitors, you know. That is, she competed with him. He didn't compete with her. He didn't have to. When things were flying for her, everything was great between them. But when things began to fall apart for her, she started to resent his success. He's a tough guy—he was a tough guy—to compete with. He humbled all of us. He was a bloody genius. We had to just put him in a separate category and forget about it. We did our own thing. But she couldn't.

"That's why my wife left me, you know. It's a phenomenon of the nineteen nineties. A kind of twist on sibling rivalry. You used to have little housewives at home, dutifully cooking and cleaning and doing their business, while the husbands were out hunting the wild beasts. But now you've got wives who are professionals in their own right. And they compete with their husbands. And any time—wait a minute. I'm going into some kind of rant here. That's—forget that. The point is that when she turned out a failure, Dianne resented Chris's success.

"And then to make things worse—he told me this some time ago—he was going to leave her. And I'll tell you why in a second. But here's the thing. Not only had she begun to despise him for his success, but on top of that he was going to throw her over. He told me that he'd told her that. He said she went into a rage, smashed things, screaming and so on. Why was he going to leave her? Because he discovered *she* was having an affair." He looked for a reaction from Stark, but saw none.

Stark said: "Who was she having an affair with?"

"I don't know. *He* didn't know. He just knew she was having an affair. My wife did the same thing. It's not hard to spot. Activities change suddenly. Business meetings that last well into the night, even weekends. Long-established routines disrupted. It's pretty easy."

"Mmm." Stark finished the last of his Scotch.

"Refill?"

"No, that's—that's fine. Lovely stuff, by the way. So—but apart from that—that's the *only* reason you think she might have killed her husband?"

"Look, as I say, I'm only suggesting that if anyone—" He held both palms up.

Chapter Nineteen

Homer Wingate was arguing with Sid Holtzman, extolling the virtues of Montreal bagels over Toronto bagels. Homer had lived in Montreal until he was seventeen, when his father had been transferred to Toronto.

"Montreal bagels are real bagels, not these big pillow things you call bagels. Montreal bagels taste richer. Probably better quality ingredients."

"I get my bagels fresh daily from the best bagel bakery in town. Up the top of Bathurst there. He's a small outfit, makes the bagels all night, delivers them himself, the guy, or his son. Ingredients schmingredients. What do you know from ingredients? You couldn't get better ingredients than is in these bagels I serve. And those Montreal things— they're too skinny. The only thing you can do with 'em is spread 'em with cream cheese. That's fine, you want cream cheese. But lots of my customers, they want ham or sliced turkey. They want a real sandwich, and for that you need good Toronto bagels. They're the best. Now, Montreal boy, you want to talk about pickles?"

"Let's talk about coffee, Sid," Stark said, entering the café. "It's freezing out there. I need something hot and strong."

"Well, Joyce is strong at least," Homer said, snickering, eliciting an angry glare from his partner, who had been completing a report on a traffic accident they had just investigated on Lee Avenue, ignoring the jousting between Homer and Sid.

"I don't appreciate your smart-ass remarks, Wingate. I told you before, that's harassment. Keep it up and I'll report you."

"Lighten up, Lee, for Christ's sake, and, Homer, why do you do it? Keep your mouth shut. She *is* your partner."

"Not for long," Homer said. "She's put in a formal request for a change in partners—incompatibility."

"Sounds like a petition for divorce."

"Listen," Lee said. "I don't want to be talked about in the third person while I'm sitting here."

"We weren't talking *about* you," Homer said. "We were talking *with* you. I mean, what the hell—let's change the subject. Please."

There was silence for a moment, and then Stark said, "You know something—this is a twist for a cop—I think I'm being followed."

Joyce perked up. "Followed? Do you have any idea who it is?"

"I have a suspicion, yeah."

"Well, it can't be your ex-wife," Sid put in. "You ain't got one. Now, if it was me, I'd know right away it was my ex. Or some private eye. She'd be looking to see if I was pulling in more dough. One time I—"

"Who do you think it is?" Lee asked. "Can we help?"

"Joyce is writing the promotion exam. She wants to wear a suit," Wingate said.

Stark glowered at him. "No, I don't think you could help. Actually, it's a little black car. A Honda Civic. To be honest with you, it could be a little paranoia."

"My ex-wife had that," Sid said. The three of them turned and stared at him. "What?" he said, raising his hands.

"I've seen the car three or four times," Stark said. "Or at least, I've seen a little black car three or four times today. I was downtown. I went to look for something in the evidence locker. I saw the car there, down the street a ways, parked where it shouldn't have been parked. I wouldn't have noticed it, except, when I saw it, it triggered a mental picture, a recollection of having seen a black car in the mirror all the way down there.

"Then I went to the store where I buy my cigarettes, and I thought I saw it down the street from there. And then I drove down to the Exhibition grounds and parked there. I do that sometimes. I was sitting there thinking about this case, looking out over the lake, trying to put it all together."

He paused, distracted momentarily, then went on, "I saw the car there again. A couple of minutes ago, I thought I saw the same car driving along Queen. Couldn't see who was driving. Anyway, what's the point of following me? I can't see it coming to anything. If they want to waste their time—" He sighed. "Sid, where's that coffee?"

"Right there on the table beside you."

"Oh, sorry." He took a sip. "Mmm. It's fresh."

"Of course it's fresh. My coffee sits for more than fifteen minutes, I dump it and make a fresh batch. It's the only way—"

"Yeah, thanks Sid." Stark lit a Gauloises. Lee leaned back from the table.

"So, who do you think it is—following you?" she asked.

"Oh, I know who it is, if it's anybody and I'm not just imagining the whole thing. If it's anybody, it's a goon working for a guy called Cataldi, Salvatore Cataldi."

"I think I've heard that name," Lee said. "What's it about?"

Stark shook his head. "Nothing to bother yourself with, Joyce. Forget it."

Lee made a disappointed face.

Stark looked at Sid. "That little supermarket across the road—most people around here shop there?"

"Oh, yeah. It's very popular. Abate's. You spell it like 'a bait,' but you pronounce it like 'a bat ee'. Gino Abate, he owns it. Nice fella. Him and his wife—now what's her name? She never comes in—"

"Well, I'm going to make a stop there."

"They got good stuff—"

"Nice coffee, Sid. I'll see you later."

The wind bit into Stark's cheek as he waited for the traffic to clear on Queen Street. He'd read in the paper that they were expecting it to be the coldest day of the winter—thirty-five below with the wind chill—Toronto cold, damp cold that gets into your bones. The cold didn't bother Stark, but he hated the wind. He always imagined that it was directed at him personally. As if nature were saying, "Cold doesn't bother you, eh? Well try this—"

As he entered the market, somebody said, "Cold enough for ya?" The speaker couldn't have been Gino Abate. He was too young, a kid, maybe eighteen, with an inane grin. Lanky, fair-haired.

"Yeah, it's pretty cold out there."

"Just as well." This voice came from behind him. A short man, dark, curly hair, mid-fifties. This undoubtedly was Gino.

"Why's that?" Stark said, smiling politely.

"'Cause if it was cold in here, it'd freeze all my fruit." Gino chortled at his joke. Stark nodded and affected a chuckle.

"You must be Mr Abate."

"That's right. I own the joint. What can I do for you? I gotta warn you, if you're selling something, I'm probably not buying."

"No, no. I'm not selling. A friend of mine, Sid, across the street. He said you run a nice market here. I thought I'd just take a look around, see what you have."

"Help yourself. Take your time. We got the best, and good prices, too. You need a hand, Billy here'll be glad to help you. Right, Billy?"

"Sure."

Abate walked away toward the back of the store, and Stark turned and smiled at Billy.

"So, Billy, you worked here long?"

"Couple a years."

"You must know a lot of the customers."

"Oh yeah, I know lots of them, most of them. I even know their names—some of them."

"You know a lady called Johnson, Dianne Johnson?"

Billy screwed up his face in thought. "I don't think so."

"Do you deliver stuff, Billy?"

"Oh yeah, that's part of my job."

"Well, this lady lives right around the corner, on Carson Avenue, top floor of a big house. Here's her picture." He fished the photo he'd taken from the apartment out of his pocket. "This is she and her husband. His name is Harper, Chris Harper."

"He was the man that was murdered."

"That's right. He was."

"I know that lady. She shops here all the time. I carry her packages home. She's a good tipper."

"That's good. So, when it's heavy stuff, you carry it, is that right?"

"Yep."

"So maybe you have an idea of what Ms Johnson bought on a regular basis. Do you think you can remember?"

"I think so."

"Good, because I want to ask you about that—"

****

Two days later, Stark called Carol Weems, who seemed delighted to hear from him. He arranged to meet her in Carbo's at nine o'clock. He got there at eight and was on his third beer when she arrived.

"God, it's cold out there," she said, unwrapping a wide, fluffy scarf from her head and neck and shaking her long, black hair, strands of it catching Stark on the cheek. He helped her remove her overcoat, delighting at the perfume wafting up from her neck.

"What's that lovely scent?" he said.

"Allure," she said, stretching the last syllable.

"Delightful. What do you want to drink?"

"You know what I'd like?"

"What's that?"

"Something my Irish mother makes. Hot whisky. Do you think they know how to make it?"

"In a Greek joint with an Italian bartender, I doubt it."

"It's easy. I'll tell the bartender. What's his name?"

"George."

She was back in a minute. "He'll make them. Hot toddy, he called it. I ordered you one, too. Is that all right?"

"Sure." He smiled. "Look. I don't want to mislead you, Carol. This is kind of a double-whammy."

"What do you mean?"

"Well. It's a date, but it's also sort of—work. I want to ask you a favour."

She looked put out. "What sort of favour?" she said

flatly.

"I want you to interview somebody for me. It's a woman, and I think—well I want it to be sort of informal. I think if we do it right, we can get the right result."

"Uh, you'll have to—"

"It's the Johnson woman."

"The one whose husband was murdered?"

"Yeah."

"What do you want me to do?"

Morty came back from a long pee break and slid on to the piano bench. "Ah, you have a lovely companion with you now, Harold. I believe I've seen you before," he said to Weems.

Stark reminded Morty of their previous meeting. Morty nodded politely, but was really not interested. He was in the middle of an argument with Ulysses, and halfway through Stark's reintroduction, when he nodded a dismissal and began playing "You Picked a Fine Time to Leave me, Lucille," in corny, exaggerated fashion.

"What the hell's that?" Stark said, chuckling."

Morty didn't answer and Stark inclined his head knowingly to Weems, who gave him a blank look.

"I said, what do you want me to do?"

"Listen, don't be pissed off, okay? We'll get this business out of the way, and then—"

"Tell me what you want."

Stark shook his head. "Look. I figure she may have killed her husband."

Weems screwed up her face. "How the hell could she have done that? She was locked in the pantry, remember? There was no murder weapon. Unless she had an accomplice—"

"That *is* possible. But not necessary. I'll tell you

how—"

Sharon put two glasses wrapped in paper napkins on the bar. The fumes of the hot whisky rose in the steam from the glasses.

"Wow. That smells great," Stark said, and Weems smiled. They both took a sip, and she nodded.

"Good, eh. It's easy to make. It'll put hair on your chest."

"Good. It'll match the hair on my palms. I hope it doesn't have the same result on you."

She laughed. The whisky seemed to relax her. "Morty—" she said. He looked up. "Stop playing that shit. Play something nice. You're too good for that crap. Forget that—what's his name?"

Morty smiled, "Ulysses J. Asshole. Okay, how's this?" He began playing "My Romance."

"That's better," Weems said.

Stark was gulping the hot whisky. "This is great," he said. "I think I'll have another."

"Me, too," Weems said.

****

It was one a.m. before they began to talk about Dianne Johnson again. They'd been in Stark's bed for an hour, and this time there'd been no loud moaning. He didn't know whether he should be pleased or not. Weems broached the subject:

"So what makes you think she killed him? I thought you arrested Bishop, the partner?"

"I made a mistake."

Her eyebrows lifted. "Well that's something. I'm impressed. The great Harry Stark admitting that he was wrong."

"It happens. Not very often, by the way. And that's

203

why I want you involved this time."

"Why? You don't think I make mistakes?"

"No, it's not that. It's just—well, let me explain."

"Please do."

Stark told her what he had learned—about the threatening letter, about the anonymous note left in headquarters, about the motive, about the Harvey woman's saying that Bishop and Harper were lovers.

"It could still be Bishop. He's got a damned good motive, too. But—I don't think so. Not anymore. You see, I figured out how she did it, the weapon she used. It was the weapon that pointed the finger at her."

"What was the weapon?"

"I'm coming to that."

Weems shrugged. "So, you think she faked it all, that she locked the door to the pantry and then went up the inside stairs, and you think she left the note at headquarters? I don't understand, why would she do that? Why would she point the finger at herself."

"She's in the ad business, marketing, some kind of consultant. In the business, they call her Too Smart."

"Why'd they call her that?"

"Too Smart as in too smart for the mere mortals in the ad agency where she worked. She went out on her own. She had some kooky ideas that backfired, and now she can hardly get a client to look at her. I think she was too smart in this, too. But maybe that's unfair, because it was really quite brilliant."

"How do you figure?"

"Well, if she'd just killed her husband and said it was a burglar, eventually, who would we have concentrated on? The burglary thing was pretty thin."

"We'd have investigated her, I guess."

"Exactly. And if, in our investigation, we'd discovered the stairs beneath the pantry floor and the other entrance?"

"We'd have thought she had done it. But what about the other entrance? Have you asked her about it? Why wouldn't she have gone down the stairs and escaped from the pantry? How could she explain that?"

"I asked her about it, and she said she didn't know the stairs existed."

"But you say she left the note—I'm sorry, I still don't understand."

"She left the note as part of her trying to point the finger at Bishop. Too Smart again. If you want people to believe that something they encounter is real, is true, what's a good way of doing that?"

She shook her head. "Tell me."

"You let *them* discover it. You don't lay it out with a big finger pointing to it, or they'll think it's planted. But if they have to find it for themselves—"

"I guess so, but what did she do exactly to finger Bishop?"

"Well, the bootprint was the most obvious thing, the only obvious thing really. Then she got really subtle. In the pile of newspapers in their recycling box, I found a local paper with an article about me. She must have figured that, with any luck, I'd be the one who got the case, my living right nearby and so on. And she'd have read that I fool around on a computer from time to time. In fact, the article was a little overblown. I really know bugger-all about computers. I use the one here to type reports and send e-mail and faxes. Saves me having to see those jerks downtown all the time.

"Anyway, if it hadn't been me, somebody with half a brain would have had a look through Harper's files and through the files in the computer and probably would have done the same thing I did, and that was to get Bobby Payne to do his magic. That's where the big finger lay—in the computer. In a file that was killed, which made it even more suspicious. Why would Harper have killed the file? He wouldn't. But somebody who didn't want the file found would."

"You're talking about these files. I don't know anything about them. What's the story with the files?"

"There was a whole bunch of reports and charts and things about a mining site in New Guinea that a company called Delsim has the rights to. What they said was—I found this out by taking them to an expert—was that the site was no good, there was nothing in it. But when I checked with the stock-market people, they said they were suspicious because the stock of this company was going up, and nobody knew why—except that BH Exploration Consultants—that was Bishop and Harper—had prospected—or whatever they call it—the site. Their reputation was so high that that was enough to push up the stocks. Now along with the reports in the computer, there was a letter from Harper to Bishop threatening to expose him."

"You want a drink?" Weems asked. She stood up from the bed and put on her panties. Stark watched her small, firm breasts bob as she walked to the bedroom doorway and turned around.

"Yeah, let's go out to the kitchen," he said, pulling on a pair of boxer shorts and slipping into a long robe before he joined her. He dug a pair of pyjamas out of his dresser and took them to her. "You want to put these on? It's a bit chilly in here."

"I'm not staying," she said. "My car's down the street,

and I have to be in at seven."

"Shit, you sure you should have that drink?"

"I'm having Coke."

"Good idea."

"I will put those pyjamas on, though. What about you? Coke?"

"No, I think I'll have a cognac, actually. You see the big fat bottle there, that's it."

"So, this letter from Harper. How was he going to expose Bishop? Expose him for what?"

"Well, not so much expose him as expose the fact that his investigation of the Delsim site was negative. Delsim wasn't releasing the results. It was obvious that if they did the stock would fall. BH's reputation was at stake, and he was insisting that the report be released or he would do it himself. Bishop isn't clean in this. There is a scam, involving a mob slob called Cataldi."

Stark told her about being conked by what he suspected was Cataldi's muscle, about the computer's being cleaned out, about his visit to Cataldi's office and about Bream.

"But wait a minute. You said you figure *she'd* killed the files? What were *they* doing?"

"Well, they had no way of knowing that I'd already seen the files, and printed them out. She killed the files to make it look as if somebody who didn't want them seen had done the killing: in other words, Bishop. She had to count on the fact that I would—or somebody would retrieve the files that were killed. It's pretty standard stuff, really. Anyway, they had their own reason for killing everything in the computer, and it had nothing to do with the murder."

"So Bishop is in on it, the scam at least, and this

Bream, he looks like a victim."

"Yeah, or Bishop could be a victim, too. I don't know."

"So the Johnson woman knew about this and saw an opportunity to bump off her husband and lay the blame on Bishop."

"Yeah, the boot?"

"What boot? Oh, the footprint?"

"I knew as soon as I saw it that no break-and-enter guy had made it. First of all, what break-in artist wears big boots like that? Secondly, I knew it was something pretty high-tech and expensive, and it was. Those boots are called Mountain Quest and they're three-seventy-five a pair. That's almost more than I paid for my last car."

"And Bishop owns a pair of these boots?"

"Right."

"But how did she get hold of it?"

"Her husband had an identical pair. They probably bought them at the same place at the same time and wrote it off to the firm."

"So she used the husband's boot to make the print."

"But she was careless, and left her husband's boot easy to find in their garage storage cupboard. At first I almost dismissed the bootprint, thinking her husband must have made it. But then, I thought, he wouldn't wear it into the house and then come back out and put it in storage. Not if he was wearing it as a winter boot. And then later, and not till after I'd accepted that Bishop didn't do it, I thought, wait a minute, what Yuppie would wear heavy-duty hiking boots on the streets of Toronto, anyway? So I think Too Smart outsmarted herself there. And something I didn't tell you about, something else in the computer."

Weems smiled. "Tell me," she said.

"She left a letter that appeared to have been written by her to her husband. A letter that said she knew he was going to leave her and she would sooner kill him and herself than let him go."

"Jeez. What was the point of that?"

"She's pretty good at psychology, I guess, although she doesn't seem to be too good at it in her work. While she was pointing the finger at Bishop, she wanted to make it look as if *he* was pointing the finger at her. If Bishop could get into the computer to hide the files, he could get into it to write a letter that was supposed to come from her. That's the thing about computers. They're anonymous. The only thing you really know for sure about something that was written on a computer was that it was written on a specific computer and then only if you're actually looking at that computer—and even then, you can't be sure."

"I still don't understand how leaving the note at headquarters could help her."

"Well, she's subtle. Convoluted. The idea was—at least in my theory—that I was supposed to think that Bishop had written the note. It was pretty ham-handed, and of course I wouldn't suspect that she'd write a note incriminating herself, would I?"

"I suppose not."

"No. So, what else? She lied about being in Ottawa for the weekend."

"How do you know that? We checked it out, and her friend said she was there."

"Her friend lied. She spent the weekend at Blue Peaks ski resort. I checked with the concierge. She goes there quite often, stays with a girlfriend, he said. Guess who this girlfriend is? Christine Harvey."

"The one who told you that Harper and Bishop were

lovers?"

"The same. She also told me that she thought Bishop had killed Harper."

"You're kidding."

"And, guess who's now moved in to the family homestead on Carson?"

"Christine Harvey."

"Remember I said Johnson was having an affair."

"You're kidding? With a woman?"

"Looks that way."

"Isn't that funny? That'd be the safest way for a woman to have an affair, wouldn't it. Lots of women go away with their girlfriends. The husband would never suspect they were diddling each other."

"I think a lot of husbands wouldn't even count it as an affair. Lots would get their rocks off on it. Unless of course the wife decided she didn't want to have anything to do with men, period. Anyway, guess what Christine Harvey—oh you don't know who she is, do you?"

She shrugged.

"She's a geologist, and was supposed to be a friend of Harper's. She was there on the Saturday night. She must have driven down from the lodge for the party and driven back again. And what supports that is the meal bill. A little arithmetic told the concierge that only one person ate at the lodge on Saturday night. Now, you asked before about an accomplice. But she wasn't there for the killing, because she spent Sunday night at the lodge—again the bills show that—she had dinner there—and she stayed and skied the next day. But she was an accomplice in one way, although I could never nail her for it."

"What way's that? You want another drink?. I'm going to make some coffee."

"I'll have a coffee. Well, because she told me that he and Harper were lovers and that Bishop had killed him."

"Oh, right. You know, there's one big thing left that you haven't explained." She handed him a mug of instant coffee. "You drink this stuff all the time? Don't you have any good stuff?"

"I don't have an espresso maker, baby, sorry. There's a drip machine in the cupboard somewhere. I can't be bothered making that stuff for myself. I just use the instant. Anyway, what's the big thing?"

"Nothing. I don't like instant all that much, that's all."

"No, no. I mean, what's the big thing I haven't explained."

"The murder weapon, buddy. You haven't told me what it is yet."

"Right. That's Too Smart again. She is brilliant."

"You keep saying that, but you seem to have outsmarted her."

"Not yet, I haven't. Anyway, the murder weapon—I went to the evidence lockup and I looked at all the pictures that were taken of the place. I spread them all out on the big table, and I looked and I looked and then I saw it."

"You're making this a bit dramatic. This is like your big scene."

"Yeah. Don't spoil it. Let me tell it this way. I went to the grocery store where she does her shopping. It's just around the corner, so I figured she'd use it, and she does. The kid in there, who's a little bit on the slow side, told me that on the Friday before the Sunday when the husband was killed, she bought a big bag of ice cubes."

"Ice cubes?"

"Mmm. Ice cubes."

"What? Did she freeze him to death?"

211

"No, no. Ice cubes stick together in the bag. They're heavy. They've got sharp edges—"

Weems looked incredulous. "You couldn't—a woman certainly couldn't swing a big bag of ice cubes hard enough to kill somebody." She frowned.

"Ah, not if you pick the bag itself up and swing it. But what if you—and they have a whole cupboard full of these—they sell them at the grocery store—what if you put the bag, not the whole bag, but say half the bag, in one of those string shopping bags. You know the kind?"

"Yeah, I've got one. I'm very ecological, you know."

"I hadn't noticed. You put the ice bag in one of those net things and you swing it. It's like a giant black jack. I tried it. It works. See the dent in the wallboard there? You come up behind somebody. You get the thing swinging—" He clutched his hands together and swung them in a big circle— "—and whammo."

"My God."

"Yeah, and the beauty of it is, what if he turned around and saw her. And said, 'What are you doing?' She could just say 'I'm just fooling around. I bought some ice at the store.' She didn't have to, because he didn't turn around, and she had to hit him only once. She'd be pretty strong—all that skiing and bike riding and everything. Probably works out, too."

"What a way to kill your husband."

"Hate. Envy. Throw in sex. Fear that he was going to leave her. She'd have nothing. He'd have to give her some settlement, of course, but not what she's going to get—or thinks she's going to get from his insurance policy. I checked. Two million bucks. He was worth about half a mill already. And he had the potential to earn a hell of a lot more, so they got a big policy. Bishop gets the same amount, by the way. Business policy. That's another reason I suspected him. So, she hits him with the ice bag, empties it into the toilet, throws it on top of the bottle in the wine bucket, hangs the string bag back up and hightails it down the stairs and up the inside stairs into the pantry. My guess is that she knew the sister was coming over later. Somebody had to find her in the pantry."

"That's amazing."

"Yeah, it is, and bloody brutal. I want her, but I don't know how to get her."

"Sounds like you've got a lot."

"Yeah, but there's nothing concrete. Especially since I was stupid enough to arrest Bishop in the first place. The Crown wouldn't go for it. I'm not going to waste my time telling them. My only hope is that she'll crack. And that's where you come in."

"I was wondering when I was going to come in."

"What I want you to do—and I'm asking it as a favour, because I want you rather than somebody else, and I could have you seconded to me, but I wouldn't do that. So as a favour, I want you to interview her—in her home. I want you to be commiserating, understanding, buddy-buddy, but with an underlying tension and underlying threat. Tell her you've come on your own hook. Tell her that I've got some real hard evidence, that I'm a really tough guy, that she'd be in for a really rough time. Get her to give herself up. Tell her mitigating circumstances, whatever. That it would be a lot better for her if she came in herself. Tell her she wouldn't do much time—and she probably wouldn't. Get her to confess. Think you can do it? Will you do it?"

"I can do it." She shrugged. "Sure, I'll do it. Why not? But you'll owe me."

"Sure. Whatever you want. Within reason."

"I want to move in with you."

"Who-o-o-a-a," Stark said, arching back.

"I'm kidding," Weems said after a time, sighing. Stark didn't notice. "I'll think of something," she said.

"I'll bet you will."

Chapter Twenty

The 52 Division cop Tilman called Stark about eleven. The phone had rung earlier. Stark hadn't answered it. A message said the inspector wanted to see him. Tilman had spoken a couple of sentences before Stark stopped him, asked him to wait, went and splashed his face with water, shook his head, tried to remember who he was and where he was and what day it was, and picked the phone up again and asked Tilman to repeat what he'd just said. Tilman said he thought he'd like to know, because it was still his case, that the two skinheads had changed their minds and now said they didn't kill Chilly. And since it seemed they hadn't actually been properly told their rights and didn't have a lawyer and so on, the Crown felt the confession was probably useless, and the Crown wanted to know where Stark was and why wasn't he investigating the case, if it was his, and why he hadn't talked to him about it.

The inspector had something similar to say, and repeated a familiar speech about Stark's being a cowboy and about how the department ran on teamwork and how dare he arrest a fine upstanding businessman like Shane Bishop without consulting him, and that he shouldn't be bothering people like Salvatore Cataldi, who was a big name in the Italian community and had no criminal connections.

Stark smirked at that, and that made the inspector

even madder, and he shook his finger at Stark, and said if he was implying anything he'd better come out and say it, and Stark said he was sorry and that he'd try harder.

"What about this dead wino? Are you on this case, or not?"

"Why don't you give it to somebody else? Obviously, the punks did it. They've got Polaroid pictures, for Christ's sake."

"Don't take the Lord's name in vain in my presence, Stark."

"Sorry." He knew the inspector was a lay preacher in some fundamentalist church.

"They say they found the fellow already dead, and took the Polaroids for bragging rights. I don't know. They probably did it, but do you want the case, because if you don't—"

"No. I don't want it. I'm still working on the Harper case."

"I'm going to take you off that case. You've messed that up. I want you to write an apology to Mr Bishop, and deliver it personally."

"Look—"

"You look. I'm telling you—"

"Okay. I will. I'll apologize, but don't take me off the case, not yet. I've just about cracked it."

"Tell me about it."

"If you don't mind, I'd rather not."

"What do you mean, you'd rather not?"

"Look, I'm sorry, Inspector. I promise I won't do a thing without consulting you, but my investigation isn't complete yet. I've just got one more thing to do, and then I promise—I *promise*—I'll come in and tell you all about it—before I make *any* move. And don't worry, there's nobody *sensitive* that I'm investigating."

"Sensitive. Why would I care about sensitive? The chips fall where they may in this department. You've got two days. That's it. Two days. Forty-eight hours. Get out of here."

****

Weems found him at Holtzman's, sitting in the back booth, staring anxiously at nothing, cell phone to his ear.

"Where the hell is she?" Stark was saying.

"I think you'll make contact real soon," said Sid, nodding to Weems.

Stark looked at Sid and caught Weems in the corner of his eye. "Jeez. I've been trying to call you all morning."

"All morning? It's nine o'clock."

"I called you last night, too. Don't you ever answer your phone? Or check your messages?"

"I was busy?"

"Busy? Busy doing what? I hope you did what you were supposed to do?"

"What I was supposed to do?"

Stark rolled his eyes.

"I thought I was doing it as a favour—isn't that what you said?"

"Okay. I'm sorry. So—did you?"

"I did," she said. She slumped down beside Stark and sighed. "And it wasn't bloody pleasant, let me tell you."

Stark shrugged. "These things never are. So what happened? Say, Sid—"

"Sure," Sid said, sliding out of the booth. "I've got a bunch of dishes to wash. But first let me get you some fresh coffee."

217

They waited till he had returned with the coffee and left again.

"So what happened?"

"I had two of them screaming at me, is what happened. That Harvey woman, wow. What a bitch. Threatened to punch my lights out. Called me, and I quote, 'a cocksucking, dog-fucked slave bitch of the rapists.' Somehow, I don't think she likes men. Anyway, I don't think Johnson did it."

"Sure she did it—okay, why not?" Stark shook a cigarette out of the Gauloises pack, accidentally flipping two others out with it. They rolled into a wet spot on the table. "Shit."

"I don't think she did it, because of her reaction. I mean she was truly shocked, but not shocked as if she had been caught, but shocked with surprise and—you know, indignation. Her mouth actually fell open. She looked really stunned. And then she got—" Weems shook her head. "She got *really* pissed off. She said she'd sue—you, not me. They both said they'd sue you. She said, why would she do it? She was going to get exactly what she wanted. He was going to leave her—"

"What about the note in the computer?"

"Well, you said yourself that she left it so you could find it because eventually you would assume that she was being set up—by Bishop. Anyway, her immediate response was, why would she leave a note like that where it could be found so easily?"

"Well, we know why. What about the insurance money? You see, I think she wanted to kill him—on principle."

"On principle? What kind of principle?"

"She hated him and his success so much, she wanted

to kill him, and the insurance money gave her the excuse she was looking for."

"Well, she says she didn't even know about the insurance money. She says she had no idea he had a policy so big."

"She *says*."

"I'm sorry, Harry—but I believe her. I've been doing this a long time—course, not *nearly* as long as you—"

He gave her an icy look.

"In my experience, suspects don't behave that way—not exactly like that—if they did it."

"You're not dealing with an ordinary suspect here, Carol. This woman is—"

"Yeah, Too Smart."

"Well—she is. I mean, she's brilliant. Cunning. She did it. It all fits. Everything points to her."

"Not quite. You had Bishop half way to the slammer for the same crime, if you recall. And that's something that bothers me. How could you shift so quickly? You had one guy you were convinced had done it, and then bingo, somebody waves a wand and you've got somebody completely different did it, and everything fit with him and now everything fits with her? Your investigation takes two weeks with him and five minutes with her."

"Because it was the same investigation. It's just that once I shifted my focus, everything came together with her, that's all."

"You're sure you're not clutching at straws?"

"I'm not clutching at anything. She did it. Anyway, you've done what you could do. I hope you laid it on thick enough."

"With a bloody trowel. I told her the next knock on her door would be you coming to arrest her, and that she'd better act fast if she hoped to get a break."

"Good. Now all we can do is wait. Trouble is I've only got till the end of tomorrow."

"How come?"

"Peters."

"Inspector Peters? What about him?"

"He gave me forty-eight hours to solve the case, or he's pulling me off it."

"Good luck."

"Thanks for the encouragement."

"Sorry, but I don't think she did it. I don't think she's going to confess. What I think is going to happen is that Peters is going to call you and dump all over you, because I think she's going to file a complaint, and I'm probably going to get into deep shit, too."

"Nothing will happen to you. I'll take full responsibility. I'll say I ordered you to do it."

"Still won't stop my boss from crapping on me from a high place."

"Look, I'm sorry if you get a little flak—"

"Never mind." She waved her hand in a gesture of unconcern. "This coffee's good, but I've got to go."

****

When Stark came out of Holtzman's, he spotted the little black Honda again, parked along Queen, about eight cars ahead of where he had parked. He set off at a run, and was immediately pushed back by a gust of icy wind from the east. He ducked his head and leaned into it. When he got to within five car-lengths of the black car, it pulled out into traffic, causing a delivery van to swerve—almost running into a westbound streetcar, which clanged its bell furiously— and a taxi to jam on its brakes and blare its horn. Stark ran back and got into his car, put the flasher on the roof, blipped his siren a couple of times and swung out in front of a flatbed truck with a load of concrete blocks. The truck's brakes squealed, it shuddered, its nose dived, shifting the load a foot forward. The driver leaned on the horn until he saw the flashing light on Stark's car, and then he slammed his hands on the steering wheel.

The black car bounced and swerved on the streetcar tracks, hugged the centre stripe and suddenly swung left across the road in front of an oncoming station wagon that was moving slowly enough that it didn't have to brake, its driver giving a tap on the horn. The black car entered Balsam Avenue and headed up the hill at high speed.

Stark had to wait for the station wagon to crawl past. When it was halfway through the intersection, he drove forward and swung wide around it, narrowly missing a parked car on the corner of Balsam.

The little car was a good hundred yards ahead, but Stark's car was faster and he caught up to it just after it had crossed Pine. He cut in front of the black car, stopping on an angle and blocking its path. The little car bumped against the curb.

Stark tumbled out of his car and dropped to his knees. His movements were so automatic, so instinctive that his gun was in his hand before he realized it. He looked at the gun as if he'd never seen it before. It felt hot, heavy, too big for his hand. His grip loosened, he nearly dropped it. Then he thought he heard the black car's door open, and instinct made his hand tighten, conditioning took over.

He jumped up, stretching his gun arm across the trunk of his car, pointing the weapon at the black car's driver. What he saw brought a wave of nausea up from his gut—his gun hand went limp, he began to shake, his head throbbed. He heard a tiny echo of little Matthew's voice, "Please, don't shoot me."

He slumped across the trunk, his face pressed against it. Sitting behind the wheel of the black car, with an expression of stark terror, was a white-haired woman of at least eighty.

Stark stood up slowly, looked at the gun dangling from his hand, considered for an instant throwing it as far as he could, but finally shoved it back in its holster in disgust. He went over and stood beside the driver's window. He couldn't stop shaking. The old lady was shaking, too, her hands frozen to the steering wheel. He'd been mistaken when he'd thought he'd heard the door open. He took a deep breath and knocked on the car window. The woman looked up, still gripped with terror, still clutching the wheel. Stark opened the car door.

"Oh my, oh my," the woman said, leaning away from Stark, her breath coming in gasps.

"Don't be frightened, please. I'm a police officer I'm so sorry. I thought you were—"

"Oh my gosh." She let out her breath. "That was awful. A policeman, yes I knew you were a policeman. I knew that when I saw the flasher on your car when you pulled in front of me. I wasn't trying to escape you, young man. I didn't see your light when you were behind me. If you'd beeped your horn, or put your siren on. I would have stopped. I didn't know you were after me. I—I know I was going a little too fast, but you didn't have to point a gun at me. Oh my gosh, I feel quite ill."

"I'm sorry. I'm *so* sorry. Please, just relax, try to relax, breathe deeply. It's all right. I'm sorry, ma'am. I thought you were somebody else. I'm really, *really* sorry about the gun."

"And so you should be. Oh my. You nearly frightened me to death. I was only going fast because my daughter is expecting me, and I was in that little antique shop and lost track of time. She's looking for a special kind of lamp. They have all these antiques in their home, you know, and I thought I might find it in there, and then I was running late, and she gets so annoyed when I'm late, because—well, I guess I sometimes am a little late—"

Stark heard the engine of an approaching car. He moved closer to the side of the woman's car. He glanced at the passing car. It was a black car, a black Honda Civic, but a CRX model, much more powerful car than the little old lady's, and it roared away, fishtailing around the bend on Balsam and out of sight before Stark could get the plate number.

"Son of a bitch," he said.

"You don't have to use bad language, young man."

****

Stark went home and poured himself a large measure of Scotch. He drank half of it in one gulp, lay on the couch and stared at the ceiling, not wanting to close his eyes, not wanting to risk the dream. But he drank the rest of the Scotch and fell asleep. He didn't dream. An hour later, he woke with a start, sat up quickly, swinging his feet to the floor, and looked around the room as if he expected to see someone standing there.

He was breathing hard and dripping with perspiration. He felt as if he'd forgotten something, that he should have been somewhere, that someone was waiting for him. He felt panic, the kind of panic he'd feel if he had a plane to catch and had slept past the time he should have left.

He shook the sleep from his head, stretched his neck, pained from having been bent awkwardly against the arm of the couch. He made a deliberate effort to get his thinking in order, to sort out what was supposed to be happening. And after a time, it became clear that there was nowhere he had to be, nothing he had to do and no one waiting to see him. His fear had been that he'd see Matthew standing in the room. He shook with relief that nothing was there. He put his face in his hands and began to sob uncontrollably.

After a time, he went into the bathroom and washed his face. He came back into the kitchen, sat at the table and lit a cigarette, blowing a long stream of smoke and watching it drift to the ceiling in the still air.

He looked at the cigarette as if there were something wrong with it. It tasted lousy. He put it out. He had a sour taste in his mouth from the Scotch. He felt like he was going to be sick. He stood up quickly, stripped off his clothes, dropping them on the kitchen floor and went back into the bathroom. He turned on the tap and spit in the sink. Then he rinsed with mouthwash and shoved four Gaviscon into his mouth. He felt something soft against his bare legs. Powder, the closet cat, was rubbing against him, which meant she wanted a drink or food, or both.

He picked the cat up and kissed her on the head, rubbed his cheek against hers. He drizzled the water from the bathtub faucet and she jumped into the tub and began flicking her tongue against the thin stream. He went into the kitchen and filled her bowl with a cheap dry cat food, the only brand she'd eat—the only thing she'd eat. She wouldn't touch canned cat food, and had no use at all for human food.

The cat swayed around the corner, keeping close to the wall, sidled up to the bowl, sniffed it, glanced at Stark, hunkered down on her belly and began to eat. Stark went to take a shower, knowing that when he came out, the cat would be back in her closet, or under the couch, or behind the drapes.

"Useless thing," he muttered, and smiled.

After he got dressed, he sat at the kitchen table and began to realize there was *another* reason for his waking feeling of unease, the nagging impression that he'd missed something. It was that the case was out of his control, that he was afraid it was going to slip completely from his grasp.

He felt he should be *doing* something, but there was nothing he *could* do. He had to wait for Dianne Johnson, and if she didn't do something quickly, he'd be off the case. And if she never did anything, there'd *be* no case. He decided that if nothing happened, he'd take what he had to the Crown. He knew they wouldn't proceed, but at least he would have done all he could, and maybe if somebody else was assigned the case and he came to the same conclusion, he'd at least be vindicated on his theory. But he knew Peters probably wouldn't reassign the case right away, and by the time he did, it would be too late. Reluctantly, with a self-pitying sigh, and as much to occupy his mind as for any other reason, he sat down in front of his computer, fired it up and began to assemble a report.

It was two hours before he'd got every supporting

detail, every observation, every conclusion in its right place.

He called Marilyn at headquarters. There were no messages. Nobody had asked for him. Neither the old lady nor her daughter had called to complain about the gun. But why did he think the complaint would get to Homicide if she did? He didn't give her his name, didn't show her his ID, and after he'd calmed her down, which was more than he'd been able to do with himself, she began to get excited about the event.

It was something she'd be able to brag about to her friends. Then he said maybe she'd better not tell her daughter, and reminded her that she had been driving a little fast, and she'd told him there was no way she was going to tell her daughter because her daughter was such an old fogey she'd get all in a flap about it. She wasn't going to complain. Why was he even thinking about it?

Chapter Twenty-One

Homer and Joyce were at Holtzman's. He told them about the car chase, leaving out the drawn gun. They got a chuckle out of it. Then Joyce got serious about the real black car. Could it be somebody he'd put away who was out to get him, waiting for the right moment? Homer asked whether it might not be the Special Investigations Unit, asking thoughtlessly, had he shot anybody lately? Then, realizing his obtuseness, said, "Oh, I'm sorry. I didn't mean—"

Stark raised a hand to silence him. Joyce glared at Homer.

"No, I told you I know who it is—I'm not worried about it. I just don't like being watched." His cell phone rang. "Now what?"

A female voice said: "She's dead, you bastard."

"Carol?"

"She's dead, and I killed her. You made me kill her." Weems was sobbing.

"Carol, take it easy—what are you talking about? Who's dead?"

"It just came over the news. It happened this morning. They said it was an accident—that she fell."

"Carol, please. Who? Fell where?"

"Dianne Johnson. This morning. Rush hour. Queen Street subway station. She fell in front of the train."

"Jesus Christ."

"I spoke to the investigating officer. He said as far as he was concerned there was no question of suicide. She got jostled in the crowd. Witness said she had papers in her hand, one of them blew away from the draft of the train, she reached for it and stumbled. She jumped. I know she did. I put the fear of God into her—the fear of Harry Stark—and she couldn't take it. She jumped. I don't care what they say."

"Jesus Christ. Where are you?"

"I'm at the station."

"What, the subway station?"

"No, my station, 55 Division."

"I'll be right there."

****

Weems was sitting in the lunch room, an untouched container of coffee in front of her. When Stark sat beside her, she didn't look at him.

"Don't sit there," she said.

"Look, Carol—"

"Don't sit there. I don't want you putting your arm around me. I don't want any patronizing. Sit over on the other side."

Stark did as she asked. "Carol, who investigated? If he says it was an accident—. I know it's a hell of a coincidence, but—"

"Coincidence? Coincidence? It's no fucking coincidence, Stark. You asshole. She killed herself because of me, and there is nothing—nothing you can say that will make that go away. If you don't mind, I'd rather you just left. I don't want any bullshit sympathy. Your case is solved. It's over. Her jumping was as good as a confession. Put it in your report. Another case solved by the great Harry Stark—with a little help from his friend."

Stark sighed. "Did she leave a note?" he said flatly.

"Yeah, she wrote it in chalk on the subway station floor."

"I mean at home."

"No, she didn't leave a note. So what? She didn't know she was going to do it. She was on her way to a presentation. She had one of those big artists' carrying cases. She was depressed—her girlfriend said she was depressed. Her girlfriend phoned me—she phoned *me*, Stark. I had to listen to her calling me every name in the book. She says it's my fault that her lover is dead. She thinks she jumped—and so do I. She did jump. The guilt, the fear—it was dwelling on her mind. She saw the train come in—maybe she even tossed the piece of paper up— as a kind of excuse, as a kind of—I don't know."

Stark opened his mouth to say something, then couldn't think of anything to say. He put his hand on top of hers, and she pulled her hand away as if she'd been touched by something revolting. Stark shook his head and left.

****

The inspector liked his report. It was neat, complete and had a tidy conclusion, and it meant no long, expensive trial.

They made no statement to the news media connecting Dianne Johnson to her husband's death. The papers linked the two events as a double tragedy. Peters chastised Stark for not telling him about the investigation.

Because he could get a cheap shot in without fear of future correction, he said that if Stark had confided in him, they would have brought her in, and she wouldn't have killed herself. Stark knew that was nonsense, but he couldn't say it. As punishment, Peters made him take charge of the investigation into Chilly's killing. The Crown was hot to nail the skinheads. They'd make popular culprits, win him points as a crusader against hate crime, and he had hopes of becoming Assistant Deputy Attorney General. It was a sure win; there was no investigating to do. Even if the confession were thrown out, they still had the Polaroids. They'd squealed a lot, said they wouldn't kill anybody, said they only smashed the guy's arms and legs, they wouldn't hit him in the head, they weren't going to hit him in the head, that they'd found him dead already. But there was no doubt they had done it and no doubt they'd be convicted. So Stark faced nothing but a lot of paperwork and court time, and he hated both.

****

Charlie Hayden called him.

"Have you been reading the papers, old boy?"

"I sometimes read the *Globe,* Charlie, but not lately. I look at Page three of the *Sun* in the local deli. That's about it. So the answer is no. And if you're talking about some article I should have read, I didn't."

"You sound awful, old boy. Something got you down?"

"Yeah, I'm a little down—so what should I have read?"

"I'm not going to tell you. Instead, you're going to have lunch with me at the club. They've got prime rib on today. A couple of bottles of red and a snifter or two of Napoleon and you'll be right as rain."

"I don't think so, Charlie. Thanks for the thought, but I think I'll take a rain check."

Hayden sighed. "All right—the news reports. Delsim. You remember Delsim, the mining company?"

"Oh, yes. I remember Delsim."

"But you're not aware of what's been happening?"

"Nope."

"Harry, if you're going to be investigating this kind of thing, you really should pay attention to the financial press."

"I'm sorry, I guess I should, so can you—"

"Well, you remember the discrepancy in the survey reports on the New Guinea property?"

"I do."

"Well, it turns out that your report was the genuine one. The second report was a complete phony."

"Oh, yeah?" Stark made a dry chuckling sound.

"Yes. And the author, one Shane Bishop—I know you know him—that was a terrible thing about the wife. Just awful. How's the investigation into Harper's murder going, by the way?"

"It's not—it's over. Person or persons unknown. Probably a burglar. What about Shane Bishop?"

"Vanished. Gone. Skipped. Cleaned out the office. Not a scrap of paper left."

"Jesus."

"And the fellow, the president, Bream. He's gone, too. Apparently his secretary was hysterical when my people talked to her. Claims he's been kidnapped. My people tell me they think she's a little more than his secretary. Anyway, he's skipped, too. In the meantime, once we revealed that the report was a phony—well, it's not really phony. In fact, it would be difficult to prove it was a deliberate misrepresentation. Actually the data were reasonably correct, barring a number or two that could be put down to error. It's just the conclusions drawn proved to be wildly optimistic after a trained person examined them fully and carefully. So I don't think there's any question of being able to prove fraud. Neither in that nor in what we suspect was stock manipulation early on in the game. I think they got away with it."

"Who?"

"That fellow I told you about, Cataldi—and his friends. They made a killing, sold when the stock was at its peak. And some company in Switzerland. We think the principal is Bishop. We've asked the Swiss authorities. For information really. So, there you are, another chapter in the sad story of junior mining stocks. Keep away from them. That's my advice. Course there's always a chance you'll luck on to a winner. Anyway, I'd better run. Thought you'd like to know what was happening."

"I appreciate it, Charlie. I do. I think it's a riot."

"I'm glad somebody does."

"Listen, I'll have that lunch with you in the near future."

****

Later that day, Stark saw a photograph he recognized from somewhere staring at him from the front page of the *Financial Post* in a street box. He hunkered down and read the accompanying story. It was all about the meteoric rise and fall of Delsim Mining. The picture was of the president, Bill Bream. Stark remembered where he'd seen him before—sitting, weeping, at the back of the funeral parlour.

Ernie Kowalski caught up with Stark at Carbo's. It was late in the evening, and Stark was sitting beside

Morty on the piano bench, singing "*My Funny Valentine*", followed by "*Moonlight in Vermont*" and "*Dancing on the Ceiling*". Ernie preferred country and western, but he smiled politely and applauded each number. He had to wait until Morty staggered off to relieve himself before Stark took a stool beside him.

"Ernie, what's happening?"

"This and that. You've got a nice voice."

"You think so?"

"Sure."

"Glad you liked it. I don't think you came in to hear me sing, though."

"No, that was a bonus."

"Yeah, right."

"I'll tell you why I wanted to find you. It's highly unlikely this has anything at all to do with your case."

"What case?"

"The murder of that geologist."

"That case is solved."

"It is? I didn't hear."

"Yeah, well, it is. The wife did it, and now she's dead, so—it's over."

"Mmm. Then I guess my information is of no use at all."

"Tell me anyway. What the hell. Hey, Sharon, bring me another and—what are you having?"

"Scotch."

"And a Scotch for my friend. So, what were you going to say?"

"Cataldi—"

"What about him?"

"Well, I told you the Mounties were keeping an eye on him for something or other. I still don't know what.

233

Anyway they called me and told me about this hooker that had showed up a few times at his office, driving a brand new BMW, must have cost a fortune."

"Business must be good."

"I guess so. Anyway, the reason they called me is they don't believe in coincidences. Neither do I, for that matter."

"What coincidences?"

"Well, the one coincidence they don't like is you paying Cataldi a visit."

"You know, this is a such a joke. My inspector tells me *Mr* Cataldi is a pillar of the community. So why would the Mounties be worried about my going to see such an upstanding businessman?"

"Yeah, well, I told you this guy has lots of political clout, lots of leverage with people the inspector's superiors have to answer to."

"You said 'coincidences,' plural. What's the other coincidence?"

"The hooker turned up dead. They found her on a sideroad a couple of miles from Cataldi's. I thought there might be some connection with the other two killings you thought Cataldi might have had something to do with. The only difference is, this is a real mob job. Piano wire around her neck. Dug right in deep. They must have dangled her like a rag doll, be like killing a child—oh, wait a minute. I forgot to mention, this hooker was a god-damned midget."

Chapter Twenty-Two

Stark was at headquarters. He was waiting to see Peters. He had his report in his hands, thirty pages. He'd included every detail, every fact, every connection he could think of that implicated Bishop and Cataldi. All the background on the Delsim business. He knew he was going to have a hard time selling the inspector on it, but he was going to use all his powers of persuasion, plead if he had to, make wild promises, do whatever he had to to get the inspector to reopen the Harper case, to let him go after Cataldi and to put out an Interpol alert for Bishop.

Peters was at a meeting with the superintendent and one of the deputy chiefs. They were talking about community-based policing, Marilyn had told him. She'd warned him that it would probably stretch into a long lunch.

"I'll wait." He sat at his desk, bolt upright, clutching the report.

"You look like a nervous schoolboy waiting to show his teacher an essay."

Stark laughed, tossed the report on his desk. "I guess you're right. You weren't going for coffee by any chance, were you?"

"No, I wasn't. Get your own coffee."

Before he could get up, another detective came over and dropped a sheet of paper in his basket and started to walk away.

"What's that, Barnes?"

"Not much. It's a report from 52 Division about that Johnson woman, the wife in the Harper case who did the half-gainer in front of the subway train."

"What's it about?"

"Read it," Barnes said with a scowl.

Stark sighed. He picked up the report. He really didn't want to read something that he suspected would be tidying up the details about Johnson's "accidental" death. It turned out to be even sillier than he'd guessed it would be. "Why, In God's name, would they issue a report on this?" It was a summary of an interview with a woman who'd said she'd been on the street outside the entrance of the subway station where Johnson had been killed.

She had called in the day after the death after reading about it in the paper. She said she'd been about to go down the stairs to the station when someone had come running up the stairs and had pushed the woman out of the way so forcefully that the woman had fallen to the sidewalk. She said she had been so shaken by it that she didn't go down to the subway. Somebody had helped her into a nearby restaurant, and later she had taken a cab home. It had happened so fast, she'd said, that she couldn't provide any identifying information about the person who'd knocked her down.

Stark made a dismissive snort and threw the paper back in the basket. After a moment's reflection, he picked it up again. "I wonder," he thought, "Cataldi?" He mused for a while, then, with a dry chuckle, said aloud, "No. I don't think so." He put the paper on the desk, tapped it with his index finger, then shoved it aside as his phone rang. It was Carol Weems.

"She left a suicide note." Weems's voice was cold.

"Johnson?"

"Yes."

"Where'd she leave it? At home? Why didn't the— girlfriend, what's her name—"

"Harvey"

"Harvey, why didn't she—Did she find it?"

"It was mailed to her."

"*Mailed* to her? What? That's ridiculous. Who mails a suicide note?"

"Dianne Johnson, I guess."

"What do you mean, she mailed it to her?"

"It's all explained in the note, apparently. She didn't know whether she was going to be able to do it. She wrote the note at home, took it with her. It says that if Harvey had received the note, then she must have made up her mind to kill herself. Apparently, she admits to killing her husband."

"You haven't seen the note?"

"No. I just got a call from Christine Harvey. She's at Johnson's place. I knew you'd want to go over there."

"Shit, I don't—Listen, you go. Hold her hand—"

"Thanks a lot. You've got to be there, though, I mean—"

"I'll be there. I just want to—I've got to think about this. I'll be there as soon as I can—an hour, two at the most. Wait for me there." He hung up before Weems could protest further.

Stark sat there, flipping through his report, underlining parts with his finger. Finally, he threw it back on his desk, leaned back with his arms folded on his chest and sighed. After a time, he opened his phone index and made a call.

****

Harvey was sniffling. Her eyes were red. Weems handed Stark the suicide note. He read it.

"It's not signed," he said.

"She wrote it on the computer."

Stark shook his head.

"You know, the thing about things written on a computer is you really can't tell who wrote them."

Harvey stopped sniffling.

"You see, Dianne Johnson appears to confess to killing her husband in this note, but I've got evidence that points in another direction."

Harvey shook her head.

"There's pretty strong evidence that points to our friend Shane Bishop."

Weems gave him a puzzled look. Harvey stared at him. "But you had to let him go, and the note—?"

"There's nothing to show that note is from Dianne Johnson. Bishop could have written that note—don't you think?"

"Well, I—"

"Yeah, Bishop could easily have written that note after one of Cataldi's goons pushed Dianne Johnson in front of that subway train. Yep, he could have. Absolutely no doubt about that." Stark interlaced his fingers, put both hands behind his head and leaned back. They were in the kitchen, sitting around the table.

"You know why Chris Harper was killed, Ms Harvey? I'll tell you. Bitterness, obsessiveness, greed. By the way, you must have known Dianne Johnson was going to end her relationship with you?"

Harvey's head snapped around. "No, she wasn't,"

she said adamantly.

"Oh. Well, unless my information is wrong, I understand that she realized it had been a mistake. I'm not going to engage in any pop psychology about it. But, my information is she was going to try to go back to her husband. I mean, back in the sense of trying to rebuild their marriage."

"That's nonsense," Harvey said.

Stark lit a cigarette. Harvey gave him a disgusted look, opened her mouth, but then said nothing.

"You see," Stark went on. "If she had been planning to try a reconciliation, Dianne Johnson could have come home on the Sunday her husband was killed with the intention of trying to persuade him to give it another try.

"Maybe she might have even told him that you were the one having she was having the affair with. He could have rejected her suggestions, and then she became so frustrated and his words angered her so much that she decided that she had to kill him. Rejection didn't sit well with Johnson. She'd had a belly full of it. If he'd dumped her, she would have known that, because of her cheating on him, and there being no children, the court wouldn't have awarded her much in the way of support.

"Now, my theory was that she *planned* to kill him. It's possible that what I just said about her appealing to him to get back together is true. It's possible that she gave him one last chance, and he didn't take it. My theory was that she bought the weapon on Friday before she went away with you."

"Bought the weapon?" Harvey said.

"Yep. A bag of ice. I'll explain in a minute. So maybe after he rejected her, she said, 'I'm going to make myself a coffee,' and he said, 'Go ahead, I'm going to have to keep on working.' And she could have gone into the kitchen to get the weapon she'd already decided on. A knife might have been the logical choice. There are some long, sharp ones in there, but Too Smart Johnson— did you know they called her Too Smart?—she would have known that a knife is not the easiest thing or the surest thing to kill with unless you're an expert. A gun? She wouldn't be into guns, and would have no way of knowing where to get one. There's poison and that sort of thing, but she wanted it to look like a burglar had done it."

Stark looked futilely for an ashtray. Finally he butted his cigarette in a plant pot, which drew an even more disgusted look from Harvey and a rolling of the eyes from Weems. Stark coughed, cleared his throat and lit another Gauloises.

"So, that's where my ice-bag theory came in. If Too Smart had planned to kill her husband, pin the crime on Bishop with the bootprint and so on, pretend she'd been locked in the pantry by the burglar—who was supposed to have been Bishop—then somehow the weapon had to be something that—disappeared, self-destructed. The ice cubes. And sure enough, when I checked with the grocery store up the street, I found she had bought a bag of ice on the Friday. My theory was that she put the ice in one of those string shopping bags and used it like a giant black jack. Brutal, but effective.

"After I began to put my theory together, I remembered finding a torn string bag in the kitchen garbage, and I remembered that the floor under Harper desk had been damp, which could have been caused by a few ice cubes' sliding under there when the bag broke.

"Anyway, that was my theory—until today. And

then I heard about the death of a woman, the murder of a woman who had provided Shane Bishop with an alibi for the time of the Harper murder and the time of the killing of a derelict—I'm sure you read about that—and I changed my mind about Dianne Johnson and went back to Bishop as the killer."

Harvey looked from Stark to Weems, opened her mouth to say something, but decided not to.

"Yes?" Stark said.

Harvey shook her head. "Nothing. You were talking about Bishop—"

"Yes, Bishop. Bishop was here all right. He had an appointment with Harper. I found a piece of paper with an 'X' on it, in the same garbage can that I found the torn string shopping bag. The paper said 'B 4:15.' 'B' for 'Bishop.' The 'X' stood for 'X-King'. I'm sure of that now.

"Bishop came for his appointment, he came in the back way. That's how the bootprint got in the snow. I'd forgotten something he told me the first time I interviewed him, that he sometimes went hiking on a Sunday afternoon. It was a cold day. He was wearing a balaclava. He and Harper were in a dispute over the Royal Cross mine property. Harper had threatened to go public. They'd had violent arguments about it before. Bishop was here, and before he could get out, Dianne Johnson arrived. He hid. When she went into the kitchen, he pulled up the balaclava, came up behind her and bundled her into the pantry. Shall I tell you how else I know that?"

"Please do."

"Because if Dianne Johnson didn't know about the trap door in the pantry—and in light of what's happened,

I believe she didn't—then the only one who could have known was Shane Bishop, who had lived in the apartment before. So the only logical one to have made the note revealing the existence of the door and pointing the finger at Dianne Johnson was Bishop. You accused him and he obliquely accused Johnson."

"And you think Bishop killed Dianne as well?" Harvey said.

"It certainly seems to add up, doesn't it? Have you got the envelope the suicide note came in?"

"Yes I do." Harvey went to the kitchen counter, picked up the envelope and handed it to Stark. He examined it. The address had been printed with a computer's laser printer. The cancellation frank was all but unreadable. He could make out Toronto, but not the date."

"Well, this isn't much use."

Harvey shrugged. She picked up a coffee mug and looked at it absently. "So, are you—going to arrest Bishop again."

"Oh, I don't think so."

She put the mug down. "Why not?"

"Well, first of all because he's disappeared, probably left the country. I'm not quite sure why, something to do with that Delsim business, I suppose."

"Well, if he killed Dianne—"

"Oh, he didn't."

"What do you mean he didn't? You said—"

"I said things pointed to his being the killer, but he wasn't."

"Oh?" Harvey said.

"No. Everything I said about Dianne Johnson's coming here on the Sunday and appealing to Harper and the rest is almost true. I'm not sure that the murder was planned, though. That may have been spur of the moment—searching for a weapon, finding the string bag, maybe putting a few soup cans in it, which would clang together and slosh around—I tried it—and then remembering the icebag."

Weems shook her head. Both she and Harvey had puzzled looks. Harvey said, "I don't understand. Then you *do* believe that Dianne did it and killed herself and wrote the suicide note?"

"Oh, no. I don't believe that. Not at all."

Harvey shook her head.

"No, you see, whoever killed Harper had to be somebody he knew, somebody who pleaded with him in much the same way I'd said Dianne might have pleaded—except the purpose of the appeal was different. Just about dead opposite, I would say. Now, before I came over here, I made a couple of phone calls. One of them was to an insurance investigator I know. He found out some interesting things for me."

Stark paused to pick at a broken fingernail.

"And I think that if I look in the file manager of the computers in the other room there, I'm going to discover that the suicide note was written *after* Dianne Johnson was killed. But the clincher in this has to do with a woman who was knocked down by somebody who came barging up the stairs of the subway station after Johnson was killed. I went to see that woman before I came here, and I showed her a photograph. You were that person Ms Harvey. You killed Chris Harper *and* Dianne Johnson."

Harvey looked as if she'd just been kicked in the stomach. Her mouth gaped. Weems looked almost as stunned.

Stark took out a police notebook, flipped to the inside back cover, and said: "Christine Harvey, I am arresting you for the murders of Christopher Harper and Dianne Johnson. It is my duty to inform you that you have the right to retain and instruct counsel—"

"You bastard," Harvey screamed.

"—You have the right to telephone any lawyer you wish. You also have the right to free advice from a legal aid lawyer—"

Harvey pounded her fists on the table. "Stop it," she shouted.

"—If you are charged with an offence—" Harvey was screaming hysterically. Weems put an arm around her. Stark raised his voice and continued with the caution until he had finished. "—Do you wish to call a lawyer now?"

Harvey was silent. Her breath was coming in gasps. Finally, she seemed to settle, took a deep breath. Her eyes went hard.

"You're a bigoted fascist prick, you know that? I knew from the moment I met you, you were a homophobic shit. You would never have suspected me if you hadn't been out to get me."

"That's an interesting concept. You know, a couple of the phone calls I made before I came here were to your colleagues. They told me you don't have a full-time job. You haven't had one for years. You work on contracts and you don't get many of those. Bad attitude, I'm told. But you like the good life. You like to ski, enjoy fine wine, travel. And you were able to do that on Chris Harper's money.

"If Johnson went back to him and dumped you, all that would end. And, even without the money, the idea of her dumping you for a *man* must have made your blood boil. And then when I found out that Dianne Johnson had a pretty hefty insurance policy—with you as the beneficiary, well—. My guess is that Dianne went back to you for comfort after her husband was killed, but eventually she returned to her first instinct. Even without a husband to go back to, she was going to dump you anyway."

Harvey had folded her arms over her chest. She was rocking back and forth, breathing rapidly. Suddenly she leapt from her chair and lunged at Stark. Weems sprung up and grabbed her in a bear hug before she could reach him.

Harvey's arms went limp, her body sagged. Weems handcuffed her hands behind her back and sat her in a chair. She sighed deeply, looked at both of them with a new, plaintive expression.

"I had to kill them," she said, "I had no choice."

****

"How did you know about the insurance policy?" Weems was entwining Stark's wiry curls around her index finger. She lay, propped on one elbow, on the sagging grey, denim couch in Stark's front room. He was on the floor, his back against the front of the couch, his long legs stretched out. He felt strangely tranquil, at peace for the first time in a long time. He had dreamt of Matthew again, but this time the dream had been different.

He had been sitting in a white confessional box, and the curtain had opened, and Matthew had been standing there, smiling. The boy had taken his hand and had led him out of the confessional and into a field of red poppies, waving in the breeze, the sky as blue as a baby's

245

eyes. He had felt Matthew kiss his hand and when he looked, the boy had gone, and Stark knew, somehow, that he would never see the boy again. He had been sobbing in his sleep when Weems had awakened him.

"The policy? I *didn't* know. I just winged it. I guessed. Turns out I was right."

"Jeez."

He shrugged.

"You were lucky with the woman at the subway station."

"Oh, you didn't know?"

"Know what?"

"The woman couldn't identify Harvey. She never saw the face of the person who knocked her down. In fact, she thought it was a man."

"You're kidding? So, if Harvey hadn't confessed—"

"It wouldn't have mattered. We'd have got her on the suicide note in the computer, anyway. I was right about that, too. She wrote it *after* Johnson had been killed."

"Tell me, what about the note that was supposed to have been from Dianne Johnson, threatening her husband? Who *did* write that?"

"That damned note. Damn, I was stupid about that."

"What do you mean?"

"All I had to do was look under 'summary info' and I could have seen when the note was written and who saved it last. That was really stupid. I guess Dianne could have written it, but I don't think so."

"Harvey?"

Stark shook his head. "You know who I think wrote that note—Harper."

"What?"

"I think he wrote it to her. After all, she was the one having the affair, and she told you that she *wanted* him to leave her, remember?"

"Amazing."

"I am, aren't I? You see—there's a failing in the language."

"What?"

"It should be 'I am, am I not?' But if I said that, you'd think I was being stilted."

"What, you? Stilted?" Weems raised her eyebrows. "So, what about Bishop and all that crew?"

"Who knows? Cataldi and his cronies will, I don't have much doubt, keep on laughing. They made their bundle on the Royal Cross scam and got out. The Securities people want to talk to Bishop about the bogus site report, but he could just claim it was a mistake and get a rap on the knuckles. You know, if Harper hadn't been killed, I don't know whether Bishop would have issued that report. I'm sure he believed that Cataldi's people had killed Chris, and that did the trick—he put the report out, as Cataldi wanted him to do. I don't think they're going to find Bishop, anyway, nor poor old Bream, the president of Delsim. I think my friend Kowalski in the Intelligence Unit was wrong about Cataldi. He's a little more of a down-home mobster than Kowalski thought. The killing of the little hooker seems to have put the exclamation point on that. Anyway, maybe the Mounties will get Cataldi on whatever they're investigating him for?"

"Why do you think Cataldi was having you followed?"

Stark chuckled. "You know, I don't think it was

Cataldi at all. I think it was the god-damned Mounties."

Weems laughed. "Come here," she said, opening her arms wide. "My poor harried Harry."

Stark climbed up on the couch. He felt something rub against his leg. The closet cat was out and wanted to be fed.

A word about the author…

John Worsley Simpson was a journalist--reporter and editor—for many years with major-market newspapers in Canada and the U.K. and with Bloomberg News. He has several published novels, including Undercut, which was runner-up to Kathy Reichs' Deja Dead as best first novel for 1997 in the Crime Writers of Canada Arthur Ellis Awards. Other traditionally published novels include Counterpoint, Shadowmen and A Debt of Death. Another novel, Death Never Says Goodbye, was published through Amazon and Create Space. He is married and lives in Barrie, Ontario, Canada with his wife, Colleen, and dog Measha.

http://www.johnworsleysimpson.info

Thank you for purchasing
this publication of The Wild Rose Press, Inc.

For questions or more information
contact us at
info@thewildrosepress.com.

The Wild Rose Press, Inc.
www.thewildrosepress.com